THE HOUSE IN THE HAZE

The house loomed far to her left, but was recognizable even under the hazy moon. The spired attic, the stately portico, the Gothic-styled windows. Under that haze, it was more a wraith than an actual structure, a phantom of grayish-white isolation.

The shadows of the past: the day when her mother hadn't come back from that drive, the harrowing experience of the trial, her father's mysterious disappearance . . . these were what it now sheltered. And, perhaps, something more, some unknown secret which, if revealed, would make the dark of memory darker still.

The author wishes to dedicate this book to the memory of Edwin Arlington Robinson, whose poetry has been a lifetime inspiration, and to thank The Macmillan Company and Charles Scribner's Sons for permission to quote from his works.

The Dark of Memory
Paula Minton

Reft of its needless riches, the dead house
Was like a many-chambered cenotaph,
Each room a sepulchre with nothing in it
But stillness and a dark of memory.

> —*Cavender's House*,
> Edwin Arlington Robinson,
> The Macmillan Company,
> New York, 1929

PRESTIGE BOOKS · NEW YORK

THE DARK OF MEMORY

Grateful acknowledgment is offered to the Dejur-Amsco Corporation for the loan of a Stenorette on which this novel was dictated, thereby freeing the author from the bondage of the typewriter.

PRESTIGE BOOKS INC. • 18 EAST 41ST STREET
NEW YORK, N.Y. 10017

Chapter One

THE GIRL who sat with her back towards the wall at the last table in the rear of *L'Armorique*, that charming little restaurant with *haute cuisine* which brings a touch of Brittany to sophisticated Manhattan, looked like either an ingenuous country girl visiting New York for the first time or a poor relation. The soft sheen of her dark brown hair, cut in a simple Dutch bob, suggested that its owner was used to shampooing it with ordinary soap and water rather than employing the glamorized and gaudily packaged beauty aids hawked on TV. There was no mascara on her short, rather thick eyelashes, and the gentle arch of her eyebrows was the result of nature, not the plucking tweezers or the shaping pencil. Her only makeup, indeed, was a slight touch of lipstick which in no way altered the candid firmness of a somewhat wide, wholesomely sweet mouth. Her slightly oval face might have served as the inspiration for a cameo, except that her cheekbones were a trifle too angular, her jaw a bit too sharply firm, and her delicately aquiline nose was marred by an irregular crookedness near the bridge . . . the result of a childhood fall.

She was of medium height, with a graceful, rather slender, figure which hinted at the excellent stock of her progenitors. The long elegant flare of her thighs, the supple, narrow waist, the gently rounded prominence of a high-set bosom, were scarcely flattered by the severe pedestrian cut of a blue cotton dress the style and cheapness of which indicated it had been purchased in the budget basement of one of the East Side department

5

stores. (As a matter of fact, it had.) Her inexpensive brown pumps were comfortably, not modishly, low-heeled, and her beige nylon stockings had durability and not gauziness to recommend them. Her fingernails were buffed, not polished, and slightly stubby; her finger tips did not have the smooth softness of those of a lady of leisure, but were work-roughened and reddened. She had a tiny brown mole in the middle of her right cheek —her tawny skin had a predisposition to freckles. And, when she smiled—which was infrequent—one observed, not so much the strong sturdy white teeth, but rather the somewhat disconcerting flaw of a badly chipped upper molar.

Her name was Lydia Turner, she was twenty years old, and the fact that she was dining at one of New York's finest French restaurants was entirely due to the dispensation of her aunt, who sat across from her and studied her with a look that was both patronizing and disdainful.

Corinne Edwards was forty-seven; she was, like Lydia, of medium height, with auburn hair piled in an impressive, ornate pompadour. That her hair as yet showed no traces of gray was the result of the expensive and fawning ministrations of her favorite stylist, Pierre, whose Park Avenue salon was visited by appointment only. Although it was an unseasonably warm May evening, Corinne wore a green brocade evening gown, and, over her plump pillow-white shoulders, a mink stole was diffidently tossed. She was buxom, but with surprisingly slender legs. A dietitian, enumerating the high-calory count of the dishes she had ordered, might have tactlessly suggested that her embonpoint was mainly the result of gluttony.

Even though her plumply rounded face with its dawn of a double chin would have confirmed this diagnosis, the ravages of good living and selfishness had not yet completely destroyed the traces of what had once been a great beauty. Her large, widely spaced hazel eyes with

6

irises flecked with green, the classic purity of her gradually arching forehead despite those telltale lines and creases which not even the most expensive beauty salon treatments could eradicate, the rounded jaw line, and the softly dimpled chin spoke of that beauty. But the small, pampered, cynically drooping mouth gave it all away.

"I do hope they won't dawdle with the service here," Corinne remarked in the throaty contralto of a woman who was used to deference and recognition. She glanced peevishly at the entrance to the kitchen, looking for their waiter. Then she turned around to stare at the other diners, and her lips tightened as much as to say: "I don't know why *they* should be served first." The girl across from her, who had been sitting quietly with hands folded in her lap, now glanced up at her companion, and, for the tiniest instant, the faint ghost of a smile crept over her lips. Then once again, as before, she meekly lowered her eyes and resumed an attitude of docile waiting.

Henri, the hawk-nosed bartender who had been a hero of the French Resistance, paused in his task of mixing a bacardi and observed to saturnine, wziened Jean, his confrere behind the bar at *L'Armorique*. "Voila une vraie Tartare!"

"Tue peux avoir raison; c'est bien possible," Jean conceded. His small deft hands were busy twirling a bottle of Pouilly Fuisse in a bucket of ice.

"I say, a Tartar," Henri insisted. "I, for one, would sooner attempt to argue with one of those *sales Boches* than to dine with Madame. *Cette pauvre fille*—so charming and so sad. She is undoubtedly the companion of madame."

Bertrand, black-haired, plump, and genial, now emerged from the kitchen and set down before Corinne Edwards a bowl of *potage tortur verte*. When he returned with a serving of madrilene, for the young brunette, Corinne, who had already begun to dip her spoon

7

into the green turtle soup, looked up frowningly and petulantly commented: "*Garcon*, I do hope they won't dillydally preparing our food. You know, we have front row tickets for *Cabaret* and we don't want to be late."

"Madame need not worry herself," Bertrand placidly replied as he refilled both water glasses and adjusted his service napkin over his left arm with an efficient flourish. "Our chef and proprietor, Monsieur Gosselin, appreciates that time is of the essence for those who wish to attend the theater, just as he knows when his patrons wish leisurely dining. I assure Madame that all will go well." Bowing, he whirled and made for the bar. A moment later, he was back with the bottle of Pouilly Fuisse. Placing the bucket on the wine stand, he first presented the bottle to Corinne Edwards so that she could verify the vintage and the year, then expertly opened it, poured off a bit into a glass, then filled her glass and stood waiting for a verdict. The woman in the green brocade evening gown lifted her wineglass to her lips, crooking her little finger and frowning as she sipped.

"Hmm, not too bad," she pronounced.

"Merci, Madame." Bertrand gravely inclined his head and moved to the other side of the table to fill the brunette's glass.

"Not too much now, dear, remember you have to be over at Mrs. Burnan's early tomorrow morning."

"Yes, Aunt Corinne." The brunette looked up at Bertrand and put out her hand to halt his filling her glass to the brim.

"Really superb turtle soup, I must say," Corinne Edwards declared as she spooned it lovingly. Her remark might have been directed at an inanimate object: in the presence of rich food and drink she completely forgot the existence of the quiet passive girl across the table from her. Her eyes shone with a narrowed intensity, her petulant lips trembled with anticipation as she raised the

8

soup spoon to them. Across the room, from behind the bar, Henri morosely nodded and muttered to himself. "Oui, j'avais raison. Decidement, une Tartare."

The rest of the dinner progressed in a similar vein of gourmandizing monologue. From the *belle sole de la Manche Glacée Tante Marie* to the *Meringue Glacée aux chocolat*, Corinne Edwards expatiated on the subtle nuances of the cuisine in a manner to give an eavesdropper the notion that she was in love with the sound of her own voice. Throughout all of this, the young brunette managed to eat her own dinner without ostentation and with an appropriate "Yes, Aunt Corinne" and "I understand, Aunt Corinne." Then, at last, after a benedictine (which Corinnne peremptorily ordered without asking her niece whether the latter might not also enjoy a liqueur), the woman glanced at her platinum-set Swiss wrist watch and gasped. "Oh, we're going to be late, I know we are, Lydia. It's such a bother having to rush dinner to make the theater. But, after all, I did promise you a treat, didn't I?"

"Yes, Aunt Corinne, and I'm very grateful. This is a lovely place, and the dinner was just wonderful. Thank you."

But Corinne Edwards scarcely heard her niece. Opening her purse, she dropped bills onto the check which Bertrand had discreetly set before her, with the gesture of one who dispenses charity in lordly fashion. Then, without so much as a backward look to see whether Lydia was following her, she adjusted the mink stole about her shoulders and forged belligerently out towards the lobby where she intercepted one of the other waiters en route to a table at the front and demanded that he go find her a taxicab.

Lydia, who had reclaimed her simple cloth coat, hastened up to her. "I'll get one for you, Aunt Corinne," she interposed. "The waiter's busy, and——"

9

"Well, really! I can see he's busy, can't I? But we're late. Oh, very well, get one then, and do be quick about it, Lydia."

"Yes, I will, of course, Aunt Corinne," Lydia answered.

Lydia turned for a moment to smile at the adorable little girl seated on the upholstered bench in the lobby, dressed in the quaintly charming costume of Brittany, with high lace cap, angel-wing lace collar, and dress resplendently embroidered with yellow broom flowers, who held a lace-trimmed cushion in her lap. As the child smiled back, Lydia's submissively sober features were almost beautiful. Then, docile once more, she went out into the street.

Chapter Two

LYDIA ENJOYED going three mornings a week to Mrs. Burnan. Letitia Burnan was eighty-one years old, with nearly all of her faculties except her eyesight. An unsuccessful operation for the removal of a cataract six years before had left her totally blind. But, in compensation, her hearing was extraordinarily sensitive and her volatile mind was a constant joy to the young brunette.

Mrs. Burnan had been the wife of a Seattle lumberman, long since dead, who had taken a prim, fearful, gangling twenty-six-year-old schoolmarm out of her neatly ordered life, given her four strapping sons and communicated his own zest for living to her so indelibly that she had retained it for the rest of her life. Two of her sons had died; a third had gone off to New Zealand to run a sheep ranch and now had three children by his beautiful Maori wife. Letitia Burnan had flown to New Zealand four years ago to visit her grandchildren, quite against her doctor's orders, and had handsomely bribed her registered nurse to accompany her on a kind of luxury vacation. Her other son, when last heard from, had just divorced his third wife and was in the process of acquiring a mistress, a painter's studio in Montmartre, and a penchant for surrealistic painting. He was childless, and his only interest in his mother was the bimonthly check which she mailed to him at various places in Europe as he moved from *amour* to *amour* and luckless venture to venture.

Della Hargell, the registered nurse who had accompanied her employer on the New Zealand trip, was still in Mrs. Burnan's employ. Of Welsh and German extraction, she was heavily set, beetle-browed, with large melancholy dark brown eyes and a tight forbidding mouth. At first appearance, she seemed phlegmatic and dour. But Lydia had learned that this was only a protective armor worn to defend her employer, to whom she was passionately devoted. Indeed, she had given up an excellent job as nurse on a Brooklyn Hospital staff to stay on as kind of general housekeeper, medical advisor, and companion. In only one phase of these varied activities were her talents negligent: she had no skill in reading books aloud, and Letitia Burnan, who had not learned to read Braille, yearned to have someone read to her as much as possible. For this purpose, Lydia had been engaged.

Letitia Burnan's inherited wealth (her husband had begun as a logger and, at the time of his death, owned three lumber mills) had been used wisely and graciously. She had invested it in government bonds and public utility stock, so that most of it was still intact in the twilight of her own life. Her only extravagances had been trust funds set up for her three grandchildren in New Zealand, a perennial library of good books (a passion, no doubt, generated by her own background as a school teacher), and, of course, the substantial checks which she regularly sent to her rapscallion son Charles.

The sprawling ten-room one-story brownstone house on McNellis Street in Riverdale might also perhaps be included in the luxury category. Letitia Burnan had bought it, however, for the strongest of reasons—to be near the only one of her sons who was still alive and in the States. For, fifteen years ago, at the time she had acquired it, Charles had just come back from London after divorcing his first wife, had married his second wife, and was earning a precarious living making collages which he managed to sell both to private individuals and to restaurants, Greenwich Village night clubs, and foreign film movies houses that appreciated avant-garde decor. And, besides, the brownstone house reminded her of the first house her dead husband had bought her in Seattle to commemorate the birth of their first son and the acquisition of his first lumber mill.

A good deal of Mrs. Burnan's money went to charitable and welfare agencies, particularly children's hospitals. She made these contributions without fanfare or publicity, entirely out of the quaintly idealistic belief that it is the obligation of those in fortunate circumstances to do what they can towards curing the ills of the world. One of her largest gifts had gone to the Hospital of the Angels in New York's teeming East Side. Lydia Turner had taken her year of schooling as a practical nurse at that hospital, passed her state board examination, and obtained her license. Ever since she had become totally blind, Letitia Burnan had asked Mrs. Davis, the chief nurse at the Hospital of Angels, to furnish her with congenial young girls who liked books and might enjoy reading to an aging woman. There had been a processional of such girls, several of whom had gone on to complete their training as professional nurses and earned the license which entitled them to practice as registered nurses who work in industry, government agencies, on private duty, or in the major hospitals of the state. Lydia had been recommended four months before when her predecessor had married a promising young intern. Mrs. Davis had recalled Lydia's enthusiasm and willingness to serve and also the brunette's habit of staying after hours while she was taking her course so that she might read stories to the crippled children in the ward.

Mrs. Burnan paid Lydia thirty-five dollars a week and her carfare on the subway from her aunt's swanky apartment on 70th Street and Park Avenue to Riverdale and gave her an excellent lunch which Della Hargell prepared. Very likely, Lydia would have accepted the assignment even if there had been no pay forthcoming.

At first, Lydia had hesitated when Mrs. Davis had told

her about the job. She would have preferred to take care of a child or an adult whose pain and suffering she might in some way ease. But, on her very first morning in the old brownstone house, she had come away deeply moved by Letitia Burnan's zest for life and impatient dismissal of her age and handicap. By now, the brownstone had become for the young girl a symbol of refuge and serenity, a welcoming place which she could enter when her mind was troubled, and when remembrance of the past was bitter gall.

Chapter Three

IT WAS hard to believe that it had happened only eight years ago. It was more like an eternity . . . like a rebirth into a new world where all values seemed to have changed and where even the language was different.

It was only eight years ago that Lydia's lovely mother had died in that strange accident. Twenty miles east of U.S. Highway 101, her Buick sedan had inexplicably swerved off the wooden bridge thirty feet above the drouth-emptied arroyo. Her mother had taken the car to drive to Santa Barbara where she was to have met Aunt Corinne. But, when Aunt Corinne had telephoned from Santa Barbara late that afternoon to learn why her sister had been delayed, Lydia's father had been alarmed and had called Sheriff Elwood Hines. And the Sheriff had called the State Highway Patrol; about three hours later they had found Lydia's mother.

She would never forget, no matter how long she lived, the look on her father's face when he came back to the house late that evening after Sheriff Hines had driven him to the place where they had found her mother. He had always been so straight and tall, with his shoulders back and his head high and a twinkle in his blue eyes specially for her . . . also, a kind of sign language all their own which no one else ever understood. He had been waiting in the big living room of the old house where Lydia had been born, and Dolores, the jovial fat Mexican cook who had come to work for them on the day of her fifth birthday (she remembered that because Dolores had baked her a special birthday cake of rich

Mexican chocolate), had been with her. Dolores had been trying to get her to eat her supper, which she wouldn't until she knew that her mother was all right. Then the door had opened and, for a moment, she hadn't recognized her father—his head was bent and his face was twisted and streaked with tears. Lydia had never seen him cry before. And he walked slowly, like an old man who tests the ground with every uneasy step; his hands were clenched and trembling.

She had been suddenly terribly afraid. Dolores had held her tightly, whispering "No, no, *querida*, you must pray to God and be brave, *pequena*." But she had torn herself out of Dolores's grasp and started to run to him, crying out, "Oh Daddy, where's Mother? Didn't you bring her back?"

And then her father had said a strange thing. He had raised his head very slowly and looked at her, but without seeing her, and he had said, "I don't know how they did it. But now they've got what they've wanted." And then he had walked past her and up the stairs without another word, and Dolores had pulled her away from the banister as she tried to follow him up the stairs. In the end, it had been Dolores who had told her that her beautiful mother was dead and that her father was so crushed with his grief and the loss of his dear love that he could not speak to her; she must be a big girl and understand and let him hide his grief alone because he was *muy hombre* and it was not good for a child to see her father cry.

And yet, very late that night, when Lydia had thought that perhaps she might go to him to try to comfort him and, in turn, have her own grief assuaged, she had crept out of her bedroom barefoot in her nightie and paused outside his door. She had heard the clicking of his typewriter. He was typing very fast, and she remembered that Mother had told her that she must never disturb Daddy when he was working on a story for the newspaper. When she recalled that, she realized that her mother would never again be able to tell her what she must do, and she had run back to her room. She flung herself down on her bed and, at last, cried herself to sleep.

The next morning Inez, Dolores's niece, who was sixteen and very pretty and worked in their house as the maid, woke Lydia by bringing her breakfast and telling her that she must dress to go with her father to the funeral that afternoon. Then, finally, her father had come to her room, his face grave and stern, and he had sat down on the edge of her bed and taken her hands in both of his and told her what she already knew. Then he had said another strange thing to her: "I may not always be here to help you, Lydia, darling, because they don't want me here and they resent me. But I swear to you before God that I shall always watch over you, even if something happens to me."

The funeral had been held late that afternoon; her mother had been buried in the family plot beside her own mother and father. Lydia's mother's maiden name was "Edwards"; the Edwards had been one of the founding families of the town of Trubecke, which was about twenty-eight miles northwest of Bakersfield and had a population of about twenty-nine thousand.

Lydia had stood holding her father's hand as her mother's casket was lowered into the yawning grave. When the minister, old Doctor Wilson, had dropped a handful of earth and pronounced the final, ominous words of the burial service, she had had to stifle a cry of pain, because her father had squeezed her hand with a convulsive strength that hurt her. Aunt Corinne had been there, too, a black armband around the sleeve of her brown satin dress. Dolores and Inez stood on the other side of the grave, both weeping loudly. And Sheriff Hines was there, too, with his towheaded, stocky young deputy Pete Ward. Several times, when Lydia looked up, she had found them both looking at her father in an extremely strange way. There had been at least three hundred people at the funeral . . . curiosity-seekers as well as people in town who had known her mother, even if only casually.

When the funeral services were over, Aunt Corinne had come up to her father and looked at him for a long moment; she then said, "If God has any justice, He will find you out."

Lydia's father had let go of her hand and he had stood looking at Aunt Corinne with eyes so darkly angry that Lydia had been afraid; then he had said, "You were always a blasphemer, weren't you, Corinne?" He had turned back to Lydia and said, "Let's go home now."

Sheriff Hines and his deputy, Pete Ward, had walked over to her father, and the Sheriff had said in an apologetic voice with a funny little smile, "I know how you must be feeling at a time like this, Mr. Turner. And I don't want to break in on you—you know what I mean. But, well, I'd like to talk to you in private when it's convenient for you—how about tomorrow afternoon? Could you come down to my office?"

Her father had nodded and said, "I'll be there. Now, if you'll excuse me." Then he had taken Lydia back to the old Plymouth which he used to go down to work on the newspaper or to drive out into the country when he wanted atmosphere and mood for his stories . . . that was how Mother had used to explain it.

The next afternoon, Father had gone to the Sheriff's office and stayed a very long time. In fact, Lydia wasn't sure that he had come back that night at all, and Dolores had given her her supper and put her to bed. Until then, the shock of her mother's sudden, unexpected death had left her numb except for the night before when she had cried herself to sleep. But now, having seen the earth shoveled in over her mother's casket, she knew that she would never see her or hear her soft gentle

18

voice again. And she cried for a very long time before she fell into an exhausted sleep.

For the next several weeks, everything seemed all mixed up and meaningless. Her father went back to his job as assistant editor of the Trubecke *Reporter*. It was summertime so Lydia didn't have to go to school, she was home all day long. In other summers, she had usually spent the afternoons playing with Beckie Randolph and Gloria Aswell, whose parents had houses a few blocks away. The three of them had been playmates all through grammar school and they had always shared secrets and games and dolls. But when Dolores urged Lydia to go out to play now, saying that her mother would want her to go on just as before, she couldn't find Gloria or Beckie around anywhere.

One day, about three weeks after the funeral, she had seen Beckie walking along on her way to the little creek which was about a mile to the south of their house where the kids used to go wading. And she had called to Beckie; she knew that Beckie had heard her, but Beckie had kept right on walking. So she had run after Beckie, caught up to her, and said, "I'll go along with you and we'll both go wading." Then Beckie had turned around and faced her and shook her head so hard that her long blond pigtails danced; she wrinkled up her face to look nasty and then said in a sneering voice, "My mother doesn't want me to play with you any more. Your daddy's wicked. My mother says so." And then Beckie had started to run away but she called back, "Don't you come near me, now!" Lydia had gone back home, crying every step of the way.

Each night since her mother's death, her father had stayed in his room and Lydia had heard the clicking of the typewriter. Most of the time, Dolores had looked after her; the few times that she did see Father, he had kissed her and told her that he loved her very much and that she must be very brave because there were things she couldn't yet understand about what had happened. And he hadn't said another word about Mother's terrible accident.

But the night after Beckie had snubbed her, Lydia had gone to Father's room and knocked at the door; she asked if she could come in. After a moment, the clicking of the typewriter had stopped; he had opened the door and taken her in his arms and held her very tightly; she could see that he had been crying, though she knew she mustn't dare let on that she knew this—not after what Dolores had said. Then she had told him what Beckie had shouted at her, and she had asked him what Beckie had meant.

Father had replied in a thick, trembling voice: "Lydia, a very great poet once said that sometimes people will shake an empty tongue talked out with too much lying, though their lies will have a truth to steer them. Someday, you'll know what that means. And I think you'll hear those lies again. You must believe in what you know to be true—and you know that I love you and loved your mother very, very much."

The next day Sheriff Hines and his deputy had come to the house and taken Father away before he went to work on the newspaper. And then Aunt Corinne, who had come back to stay with Lydia at the house, told her that her father had been arrested on the charge of murdering her mother and would stand trial in Bakersfield. Six weeks later, the trial had been held and Lydia had been called as a major witness. It had been an indelible nightmare for her . . . the agonizingly long waiting before the trial took place, the restricted visits to the jail where her father was being held until his appearance in court, the hostility of the neighbors in Trubecke.

Still a child, she had sat in court and listened unbelievingly while the prosecuting attorney had demanded the death penalty for her father. He had brought forward witnesses who said that examination of the Buick in which her mother had crashed into the arroyo revealed that the car had been tampered with. An officer of the Highway Patrol and a mechanic from a garage four miles away from the scene of the accident had both said that the steering wheel and the brakes had been deliberately damaged so that the car would go out of control at high speed.

Dolores and Inez had been called to the witness stand to testify as to whether they had ever heard Lydia's mother and father arguing or quarreling. Dolores had been very nervous and hesitant, Lydia remembered, and had finally said that once or twice she had heard them quarreling, though she hadn't been able to hear what they were saying. Lydia couldn't understand why Dolores would say such a thing. But Inez, though very frightened to be on the witness stand and often speaking in Spanish instead of English, had said that she had always thought that Lydia's father and mother had been very happy together and that she, herself, did not know of any quarrel.

When it had been Lydia's turn, she had become angry at the prosecuting attorney when he kept trying to make her admit that her parents hadn't got along, because it wasn't true; then she had talked about the night she had told her father how Beckie had snubbed her and how her father had reassured her that he loved her and had loved her mother very much. She hadn't mentioned about the poetry, though, because she wasn't sure that she had remembered exactly the words he had used, and she knew she was under oath and mustn't say anything that wasn't exactly right.

After a week, the case had been given to the jury. Two days later, the jury brought in a verdict of "Not Guilty," and her father was free. Her father's lawyer told her that her own testimony and her love had saved him, because she had helped create a reasonable doubt about his guilt, and there had been no actual proof except the circumstantial evidence of the unreliable car which only her mother and father ever used.

So Lydia had gone back home with Father to Trubecke and she had told herself that she would do everything she could to help him forget the terrible ordeal he had suffered and the terrible things she had heard some people say about him. Some of their closest neighbors had gone to Bakersfield to be at the trial, and the girl had wanted to make them take back some of the awful remarks they had made about her father's being "very clever" and "What else would you expect from an outsider and a man who married into money?"

But for all the child had tried to cheer him up, it hadn't done much good. He looked so much older and tired and sad. And he had lost his job on the newspaper; the publisher had fired him even though he had been acquitted.

Two weeks after they had come back home, late one rainy evening, Father had told her that he was going for a drive to think things over. And he had never come back.

A few days later, Aunt Corinne had told her that he was dead and that she was going to take care of her from now on. A month after that, Aunt Corinne had taken her to New York to live in her beautiful apartment. She had explained that Lydia's mother had left a lot of money in her will and that she was going to use it to see that Lydia had a new life in surroundings far away from the dreadful things that had happened in Trubecke.

Chapter Four

THERE WAS so much new about New York to make Lydia almost forget that she had spent the first twelve years of her life in a little California town, that she had really never stopped to wonder why Aunt Corinne had chosen to bring her there after the tragedy. Nor had she thought it particularly strange that their new home should be a luxurious apartment on the twelfth floor of one of the newest and swankiest high-rises. She had known, ever since she was old enough to remember, that her mother and her aunt had inherited the huge two-story white wooden house in Trubecke with its imposing portico and its low-beamed attic from their father, Jonathan Edwards. And Jonathan Edwards, her maternal grandfather, who had died before she was born, had been Mayor of Trubecke and founder of the First Commercial Bank. His wife had died two years after giving birth to Lydia's mother, Marcia, who was five years younger than her sister Corinne.

She knew, too, because her mother had told her, that Jonathan Edwards had left both his daughters a considerable amount of cash and wisely invested stocks as well as title to the house. But he hadn't built the house; it had been his father Augustus who had had it built the year he brought his month-old bride from Madeira to settle down in the then unknown little hamlet. Augustus Edwards had been a mining engineer fresh out of a new university called Stanford, the son of a wealthy Oregon wheat farmer, who, himself, had come as an immigrant from Scotland where he had been a farmer too. Augustus

Edwards had been convinced that there were valuable and, as yet, unearthed mineral deposits in much of the unpopulated area between Bakersfield and Los Angeles. On one of his ramblings through the countryside near the site of Trubecke, he had discovered deposits of copper in the low moundlike hills to the west. He had interested two of his friends from Stanford, whose parents were affluent, to go into partnership with him. Within three years, by which time the mine was completely played out, he and his two friends had become extremely wealthy.

After the partnership had been dissolved, Augustus Edwards became convinced that the Southern Pacific Railroad was certain to build a line which would run near or through Trubecke, and his personal enthusiasm and the investment of much of his own private fortune in building a school, a small hotel, and several stores had much to do with the rapid growth of the small isolated village. The Southern Pacific never built its extension as he had hoped and he died a disappointed man, leaving his son Jonathan to take up the splendid dream at the point it had ended for him. Although Jonathan Edwards believed as earnestly in that dream as his father had done, he was no more successful in realizing it, although he did manage to induce an Eastern paper box manufacturer—whom he met at a bar in San Francisco—to found a new factory in Trubecke which gave work to hundreds and brought more hundreds of workers into the town.

So the house in which Lydia had been born must have been about eighty years old. In its day, it had been one of the most beautiful homes in Northern California. It had been made of the finest cypress and redwood to be found in the entire state. Trubecke was in earthquake country some fifty miles away from one of the major California faults, and the climate varied from moderate to very warm, so there was no reason to use heavy brick or stone. With its gables, its spired attic, its portico, and its huge Gothic windows, the gleaming white front faced the east; and at its back, far distant on the horizon, were the very hills from which Augustus Edwards had mined his wealth.

What a roomy, comfortable house it had been! Twelve rooms in all on the two floors, counting the huge dining room, living room, the library, and the kitchen. And how Lydia had loved the winding narrow staircase that led to the second floor. It had always been a game with her to see how quickly she could descend without losing her balance—holding very tightly to the banister as she scampered down the stairs. The rooms on the second floor were much smaller. Augustus Edwards had hoped to have a large family, but he had been disappointed in this as he was in the realization of his dream about the Southern Pacific. His wife had given him just the one child, and the doctors had told him that she could never have another. So there were all those empty rooms; that was why Aunt Corinne had continued to live in the old house together with Dolores and Inez even after Lydia's mother had married Arthur Turner.

Arthur Turner had come to Trubecke quite by accident. Born in Chicago and a graduate of the journalism school at Northwestern University, he had been orphaned at eighteen when his parents died in a plane crash. They had owned a jewelry shop on Michigan Avenue and had been comfortably well off. Arthur's uncle, who had been appointed executor of the estate, had offered to buy the jewelry shop outright when Arthur came of age. His offer was accepted and there had been no haggling over terms. Arthur Turner had no interest whatsoever in business because his major interest in life was writing. In high school, he fancied himself to be a major poet and wrote a good many sonnets imitative of Edwin Arlington Robinson, the poet whose work he most revered.

He continued his writing of poetry at the university, and succeeded in having several of his efforts published in small "artsy" magazines and in the "Line O'Type" column of the Chicago *Tribune*. It was only when some of the vanity magazines began to write him urging him to contribute—at a price—that he wryly decided that he was not likely to become Robinson's successor. He had edited the daily newspaper in his senior year at school, and, after his graduation, took a beginner's job as a copywriter for one of the mail-order houses.

Turner continued to write, trying his hand at essays and short stories, but with very little success. Writing and omnivorous reading were his absorbing passions, for he was retiring by nature and held a candidly low opinion as to his being either extrovert or personable enough to make a success as an executive in the highly competitive business world. His inheritance and the sale of the store had left him with enough tangible means to release him from the specter of unemployment, yet he was too idealistic to lead a parasitical, hedonistic life.

Arthur Turner was almost six feet tall, with curly brown hair, glasses and serious earnest features; he was inclined to plumpness and a slouch in posture and was not especially interested in outdoor sports. Inwardly, however, Turner was an incurable romantic, and, as romantics so often are, chaste. In spite of his wide reading and his educational background, in spite of the sensible attitude of his parents in educating him about the opposite sex at an early age, his adolescence and early manhood were fraught with the tortures of the damned . . . exactly because he yearned for love while, at the same time, he repudiated it on purely physical terms. His loneliness after his parents' death—he made few friends, and those only with difficulty—augmented that torment. This, in turn, drove him all the more to express himself in writing.

After two years at the mail-order house, Arthur

Turner found a job in a small congenial advertising agency on North Michigan Avenue. He respected the intelligence of his employer and his associates, and they in turn appreciated his. His reticence and almost self-goading application to his work became virtues in the intimate office while in a larger firm they might well have indicated nonconformity. He stayed three years on that job, and the discipline to detail and to clarity of expression which it gave him was priceless. His imaginative copy and his sincere interest in the problems of the agency's clients were directly responsible for increased billings and the addition of new clients. He received several handsome raises; the money itself did not concern him, but the warm glow of recognition by people he could respect and admire helped somewhat to mellow his personality. Then, without warning, his health began to fail and a medical examination revealed that he was suffering from a mild attack of tuberculosis. The doctor recommended a warm dry climate and advised him to try to learn the secret of relaxation—he had driven himself to this illness, the doctor said, by a kind of self-scourging.

One of Arthur Turner's few friends at Northwestern had been Jim Lawlor, who had shared his interests in books and music, and who had sometimes spent many a long evening with him at a little off-campus restaurant discussing philosophy and literature. Jim had, he knew from continued correspondence after his friend's graduation, found a reporter's job on a Los Angeles newspaper. Jim had decided to try his luck on the West Coast because his fiancée had unexpectedly told him that her father was to be transferred from Chicago to become district sales manager of his hardware company's Los Angeles branch.

The idea of working on a newspaper appealed to Arthur Turner, so he wrote Jim while he was in a private hospital for three months undergoing treatment. Jim wrote back that he would make inquiries, but warned Arthur not to be too hopeful so far as Los Angeles was concerned. He, himself, had been lucky by walking in to ask for a job just a few hours after the city editor had fired two reporters for unethical practices; but it was quite possible that Arthur might make the rounds of the newspaper offices there for several years without success. By this time, Jim had married his college sweetheart and had two sons, a house near Santa Monica, and a byline on every story he wrote. Arthur Turner was never a man to envy anyone his material possessions—but it is quite likely that he secretly envied Jim the warm companionship of the latter's family.

About two months after Arthur Turner got out of the hospital, Jim telephoned to tell him that he thought he had a few leads and that it might be a good idea for Arthur to come out to the West Coast. At worst, it would afford him a pleasant vacation and the climate would certainly be beneficial. Jim was going to take his vacation and drive Marge and the kids up to San Francisco where she planned to spend a week or so with a cousin. During that time, Jim proposed that Arthur and he could drive through some of the towns in the Northern California area. Acually, one of the possible openings was in Bakersfield, and Jim had intended doing a feature story on the development of wildcatting in oil that was going on down there.

So Arthur Turner flew out to San Francisco to meet the man who was really his only friend, and by that meeting, to meet his destiny. Success hadn't changed Jim Lawlor a bit. He was still the same straightforward, humorously earnest, vital person he had always been. And Marge was a beautiful blond young woman with a level head on her shoulders and a sense of humor to match Jim's. Arthur Turner detested self-pity as a coward's resource, but, assuredly, he must have felt a twinge of it due to his own lonely state when he saw how

28

much in love Marge and Jim still were after six years of marriage.

After a few days in San Francisco seeing the sights, Jim and Arthur drove to Bakersfield. There, Jim introduced him to the editor of the larger of the two newspapers in that city and went about combining business with pleasure by getting the data he needed on the Bakersfield oil development. The editor took a liking to Arthur Turner, the job that Jim had thought was open had just been filled, but he suggested that Turner go see John Wendell, editor of the Trubecke *Reporter*. To be sure, Trubecke was a small town, but if Arthur wanted to stay in the area for reasons of health (Arthur had naturally told the Bakersfield editor his reason for giving up a good job in Chicago and wanting to settle in California) there was a very good possibility of a job there with Wendell. So Arthur Turner and Jim Lawlor drove to Trubecke, and Arthur had his interview with John Wendell; he was hired at a salary of forty dollars a week.

Turner was then twenty-seven and he had never been more lonely in his life. In Chicago, there had been the symphony orchestra, the opera, the museums, and every possible form of entertainment which the intellectual mind could desire. In Trubecke, there was one small movie house which changed shows every two weeks, a bowling alley, a small riding stable, several taverns with juke boxes, and a small library next to the public school. Getting to Los Angeles for a week end was difficult unless one had a car since there was no connecting railroad line from Trubecke to Bakersfield, and Turner had never learned to drive a car.

He had left his books and records, some prize pieces of his parents' furniture, and most of his clothing in storage in Chicago with the understanding that it could be shipped out to him within a day at his request. Very likely he had some few misgivings about making a new life for himself in a small colorless town where he was certain to be considered an outsider and where even the scenery bore little resemblance to the paradisal portraits created by the California State Chamber of Commerce with tourists in mind. His original plan was to stay there six months, then to go to a doctor in San Francisco or Los Angeles to learn whether his tuberculosis had been successfully cured. Although he was not gregarious by natural inclination, he instinctively felt that if he had to stay in California for the rest of his life, either of those two major cities would be more likely than a small town to offer him opportunities, not only for earning a living, but also for furthering the creative abilities he felt he had as a writer.

The Trubecke *Reporter* was issued twice a week—on Wednesdays and Sundays. Its absentee publisher, Matthew Carroll, owned a string of small daily and semi-weekly newspapers between Eureka and San Diego, and spent most of his time in the latter city in a palatial home near the ocean when he was not traveling to Hawaii or Europe with his latest paramour. He bought a syndicated Sunday magazine and comic section, the purpose of which was to induce the inhabitants of the small towns where his newspapers were published to be satisfied with what they had locally and not spend their newspaper dollars subscribing to the big city journals.

Depending on local advertising, the Trubecke *Reporter* varied from eight to sixteen pages. Arthur Turner's job was, not only to visit the leading residents and lesser fry of the town to get news as well as society features (despite the limited recreational facilities of Trubecke, the wealthier citizens were forever inviting their friends over for bridge and a buffet supper, and that, naturally, was worthy of imperishable mention in the *Reporter*), but also to sell advertising to the merchants and even classified ads to the local citizenry. His boss John Wendell pointed out that, if he intended to stay on the job for any length of time, he had better get himself a car, because the farmers and merchants of Clareton and Webster, towns of about five thousand population within a thirty-mile radius of Trubecke, could get better results in the *Reporter* than in the Bakersfield newspapers.

Arthur Turner set about his new job with the same dogged perseverance and enthusiasm that he had shown back in Chicago at the mail-order firm and at the advertising agency. He arranged to room and board with an elderly widow whose house was located only five short blocks from the newspaper office. There were two other boarders, both of whom worked at the paper box factory, but he had a spacious airy room with private bath, and there was a huge desk beside the big bay window where he could sit to type.

When he had met Jim Lawlor in San Francisco, he had bought himself a portable typewriter as his old battered Remington was back in storage in Chicago. He had come to Trubecke in August, the hottest month of the year—the temperature hovered steadily around the 100 degree mark. But it was a dry bearable heat. Besides, Mrs. Grantham, his landlady, had just installed a desert air cooler in the window of his room. Its only drawback was its noisiness, which sometimes bothered him when he was sitting at his desk lost in the plot complexities of a short story he was trying to compose.

After about three months, John Wendell expressed his pleasure with his new reporter and gave him a five-dollar raise. At the same time, he repeated his suggestion that Arthur Turner learn to drive and buy himself a car because the advertising revenue, especially from the two outlying towns, wasn't really what it ought to be. Wendell also remarked that he would like to inaugurate a new feature column, something with human interest and perhaps a little philosophical opinion thrown in for good measure. That evening, Arthur Turner went back to his room and wrote the first of a series of "Reportorial Reflections" which was destined to earn him both his promotion to the assistant editorship of the newspaper and a wife.

About a month after the series began, Marcia Edwards, who had driven into town to buy groceries one morning, stopped in at the newspaper office to compliment John Wendell on the fascinating articles that he had started to run in the *Reporter*. The first several articles had had no byline, but Wendell was an honest man and he told Marcia who had written them. He did even better than that—he called Arthur Turner in from the pressroom, where the latter was helping set up a display ad which he had just brought in from the bank, and introduced him to Marcia.

It was love at first sight for both of them. At least, that was what Lydia's mother had always told her. And she could still remember, back to about the time when she was ten or eleven, that she had never grown tired of asking both her father and her mother how they had met and how her mother had taught her father how to drive a car and poked gentle fun at him for being such a "mechanical numbskull."

But, numbskull or not, her father had proposed three months after their meeting in the *Reporter* office, and, in another three months, Marcia Edwards and Arthur Turner had stood before Doctor Wilson in the First Episcopalian Church and promised to love, honor, and obey each other until death did them part. And Lydia had been born the next year on the day before Christmas. She remembered how she had used to say it wasn't fair because she probably missed out on presents, considering that her birthday and Christmas were almost the same day. Then her mother would always take her on her knee and pretend to scold her for being greedy and tell her that if she were a good girl all year long, she and Daddy might just possibly pick some other day in spring or summer as her birthday so that she could have another set of presents. How happy all three of them had been together . . . her mother, slim and of medium height with that lovely wistful oval face with great dark brown eyes, and long, even darker, brown curls tumbling about her shoulders so that they danced whenever she laughed at one of Daddy's jokes . . . her father, tall and straight, not saying very much a lot of the time, but with a smile and a twinkle in his eyes whenever Lydia looked at him. She had seen them together so often in the library in the old house, sitting side by side, reading the same book, sometimes silently, sometimes reading aloud by turns . . . and there had been times when she came in unexpectedly to find them stopping to look at each other and then kiss. She had told about these affectionate practices at her father's trial.

Aunt Corinne had never seemed to be interested in men. At least, she had never got married. And she had stayed with them in the old house all the time, although she never got in their way or seemed to want to talk very much to Lydia's father. Once in a while, she would go away for a week end to Santa Barbara or San Diego, but she had her own car which she usually kept in the garage at the Hines Auto Service Center. Two years after Lydia's birth, Elwell Hines had been elected sheriff to fill the office left vacant by the death of old Henry Cortberg. When Hines became sheriff, he hired young Pete Ward, the deputy, to run the business for him because there really wasn't much law enforcement work for a deputy in Trubecke. Aunt Corinne had driven her Dodge down to Santa Barbara the week end just before Lydia's mother had been killed. Sheriff Hines and his deputy had said so at the trial. . . .

By the time Lydia was six, her father had been appointed assistant editor of the *Reporter*, which had grown to twenty-four pages for even its Wednesday edition. And, that same year, her father had had his first novel published by a New York firm. Her mother had shown her the book with its bright jacket and her father's picture on the back cover and read aloud to her the flattering things it said about him. The title of the book was *No Lost Arrears*, but when Lydia had asked her mother what the story was about, her mother had kissed her and said that it was a kind of love story and that someday she would be old enough to read and understand it. Her father had gone to New York to see the publisher; he had also sold a few short stories to a national magazine.

Aunt Corinne had never seemed particularly interested in her father's writing, and Lydia had never had a chance to read the book. She knew that it had gone out of print and that the sales had not been too great because her father had told her so. She remembered, too, that it had been about six months before her mother's death that she had asked Father if he would let her read the book and he had laughed and told her that she still had a few years to go and that, after all, she might be disappointed, because it wasn't really a very good story. She knew that he had kept a copy in the library, but before Aunt Corinne had taken her to New York and moved all their things out of the big house—either to sell them or to store them—the book had been missing.

The one thing Lydia missed at Mrs. Burnan's house was an attic. The attic back in Trubecke had been a wonderful place to play on a rainy day. There were trunks and chairs and tables and some framed pictures and an old grandfather's clock which didn't work any more but which had belonged to Augustus Edwards and was being kept as an heirloom. Sometimes, too, her father liked to go up there and take along the old portable typewriter on which he had written his first articles for the *Reporter* and sit on a three-legged stool near the window with the typewriter on top of a low squat trunk and do one of his short stories. He had sold quite a few short stories to magazines—some of them were about people who were very much like people who lived in Trubecke. She knew that, because she had once overheard Aunt Corinne telling her father that he was unpopular enough as it was as an outsider without getting people really down on him by writing stories about them that everybody all over the country could read. . . .

Aunt Corinne hadn't really been unkind to her, all things considered. She had put her through high school and given her a small allowance for spending money. Then there had been a trip to Europe. Of course, Lydia had had to pack the bags and arrange to get taxicabs and guides and do a lot of work that personal secretaries or maids usually did for their employers. And Aunt Corinne hadn't seemed to care as much for sightseeing as tourists usually do. She'd told Lydia that she just didn't dig churches and museums and art galleries and all that kind of cultural mishmash, because it was all a part of the dead past and reminded her too much of Trubecke.

Aunt Corinne liked to go to nightclubs and famous restaurants and the theater, and she was never happier than when she could walk into a posh place and call the manager or maître d' by name. Here in New York she would telephone ahead for reservations to places like The Tower Suite and say, "Now, you be sure to have Paul Kovi see that I get strawberry crêpes suzette for dessert with brunch," or The Four Seasons and insist that Stuart Levin personally see to it that she would have beefsteak tomato with her dinner that evening, or Quo Vadis and demand that Bruno Caravaggi himself supervise the preparation of her *Pigeonneau Roti Paysanne* for lunch that day. Both at home and abroad, indeed, Aunt Corinne's idea of an exciting time appeared to be gorging herself with the most exotic food and drink. It had not been that way back in Trubecke, Lydia remembered. Dolores had prepared simple meals most of the time, occasionally giving them an authentic Mexican dinner. And her father and mother rarely drank wine, and it was usually a native California vintage.

And then, of course, clothes. The closets of the Park Avenue apartment were filled to bursting with expensive dresses, coats, and hats, acquired from Dior or Balenciaga abroad or from Henri Bendel in New York. Lydia's own clothes, to be sure, had no such fancy labels. Perennially, Aunt Corinne gave her a small allowance and told her that it was valuable experience for her to learn how to stretch it out so that it would cover her needs.

No, there was no reason why Lydia shouldn't be grateful to Aunt Corinne. Aunt Corinne had loaned her two hundred and fifty dollars so that she could take her course in practical nursing and get her license, which made her eligible to take the state examination. She could write "L.P.N." after her name. She really wanted to be a registered nurse like Della Hargell, and, whenever she had a chance at Mrs. Burnan's, she would ask Della about the latter's experience in hospitals before she had come to work for Mrs. Burnan. She knew that she would need at least two to three years in a hospital school of nursing, and then perhaps a year or two in college. But the opportunities were boundless . . . Della could have become a doctor's assistant, a public health nurse, a teacher, or administrator, or research worker.

But such an education would take a good deal of money, and Lydia had none of her own. She knew that most of her mother's inheritance from Jonathan Edwards had gone to Aunt Corinne after her mother's death due to the terms of her mother's will. Under California law, her father's money would have reverted to her. The only trouble was, he had left almost nothing, and Aunt Corinne, as executrix and legal guardian until she became twenty-one, had told her that the money her father had left had long since been used up in

36

putting her through high school and furnishing her with room, board, and clothing.

Lydia knew that Aunt Corinne had a great deal of money. She must have had, in order to have all those clothes in the closets, to dine at the finest restaurants, and to have front-row seats at the new Broadway shows. But she didn't want to ask Aunt Corinne to lend her any more money, not even for tuition so that she could become a registered nurse. She didn't like the feeling of being obligated. She already felt dependent enough, and whenever she went out to dinner and the theater with Aunt Corinne, like the time at *L'Armorique*, she was made to feel like a servant useful only for the most menial tasks.

That wasn't exactly the right word, she knew. Because a servant is a person who serves, just the way a nurse serves a patient. But the difference was that a nurse is needed by the people she serves if they are sick or in pain. And the feeling of being needed by someone is one of the most wonderful rewards in the world. That was why Lydia wanted so much to go on with her nursing studies. She had wanted to be a nurse ever since the day when she and Beckie Randolph had been playing and Beckie had fallen down and skinned her knee. Beckie had been hysterical at the sight of the blood, and Lydia had torn off a piece of her dress and tied it very tightly just above the cut so it stopped bleeding. No one had ever told her how to do a thing like that. But she had felt needed and useful. Even though, a year later, Beckie had run away from her and shouted back that awful thing about her father, she would never forget how Beckie had stopped crying and stammered out, "Gee, Lydia, you made the bleeding stop! You're wunnerful!"

Chapter Five

LETITIA BURNAN was in a sardonic good humor this morning. Della had wheeled her into the library in the comfortable adjustable chair which had been a gift from Mrs. Davis of the Hospital of the Angels as a kind of thank-you for the large donations which the blind old widow had made to the institution. Letitia Burnan had grumbled and protested against the thoughtful gift, but level-headed Della had just sniffed and said, "Well, if you'd rather stumble around and bang yourself all up and give me a lot of extra trouble looking after you, don't use it, then." And Letitia Burnan had chuckled and replied, "You go to hell, Della." And from then on she was never without it. Della knew very well that her employer detested pity and sympathy and coddling, and that was why she had been brutal in her comment about the wheelchair. If she had made the commonplace remark of, "At your age, you ought to treat yourself to creature comforts," Letitia Burnan would undoubtedly have had the chair sent back.

That was another thing Lydia admired about the courageous blind woman for whom she came to read three mornings a week . . . her refusal to fall back on the all too convenient excuse of her handicaps. Gentle though Lydia's nature was—her compulsory subservience the past eight years would have indoctrinated her with such an attitude if she had not already been inherently docile—she had already drawn comparisons between her aunt and her employer—to the disadvantage of the former. For Aunt Corinne was unreasonably intolerant of

38

the slightest imperfection in her serenely perfected plans for pleasure and entertainment. Only six weeks ago, she had made a scene at Les Pyrenées and railed at Rene Pujol himself on the grounds that the Sauce Bernaise with her tournedos had been too strong and thick. Lydia had sat there through it all, her eyes lowered, and her cheeks reddened with shame, trying to efface herself. If blindness and old age had been Aunt Corinne's lot, she would long since have drowned in the flood of her own self-pity.

But Letitia Burnan was forever exchanging jokes with Della, grimly mocking jokes about her own infirmities. Although she obviously enjoyed the comfort of the wheelchair and the feeling of luxury it gave her to be moved (for although Della's words and manner invariably proffered a no-nonsense-out-of-you attitude towards her employer), she very often insisted on being without it and walking from one point of the room to another, relying solely on her own instincts. And when, as was inevitable, she would bump against the chair or table, she would chide herself aloud, saying, "Aren't you a stupid old lady, though! A baby wouldn't be half so clumsy!" Or, in almost the same breath, she would say, "God has given me more years than I'm entitled to, but that still doesn't excuse stupidity!"

Della led Lydia straight to the huge sunny room where Letitia Burnan was waiting. "She's in a good mood this morning, the old girl is." The registered nurse winked at Lydia. "Wants me to have this house when she dies, no less. And you're to have your choice of books from her library, she says. She likes you the best of any of the readers she's had so far, I'll tell you that much. Come along now, mustn't keep her waiting or she'll get out of that wheelchair and come looking for you."

"I don't like to hear anyone talk about when they are going to die." Lydia's eyes shadowed with a soft distress.

"That one!" Della chuckled as she opened the library

door for Lydia. "She'll outlive us all, you watch and see if she doesn't just out of pure meanness!" Then, in a loud bossy voice, "All right, Mrs. Burnan, you just stay still in that chair. She's here now."

"What are you two conspiring about?" There was nothing fragile or senile about Letitia Burnan's voice; though high-pitched from age, it still retained a robust volume. It would not have been hard to have imagined her as the kind of wife who took lunch in a pail out to her husband in the woods and then stayed on to wield an axe herself. As a matter of fact, she had done exactly that in the early days of her marriage.

"Well, if you must know, you cantankerous old coot," Della snapped back, "Lydia and I were figuring out what we were both going to do with the money you're going to leave us. Does that answer your question?"

Lydia sent Della a shocked imploring glance; after three months she still found it hugely embarrassing to find herself ducking the verbal cudgels which Della Hargell and Letitia Burnan swung at each other. She was able by now to sense the underlying humor behind this constant flailing away, but it still made her uncomfortable to hear Della constantly mentioning death in the old woman's hearing.

Letitia Burnan leaned back until her head bumped the back of the wheelchair and laughed until her shoulders shook. Instantly, Della hurried over to her patient, a worried look on her homely face, ready for trouble if the laugher should turn into a coughing fit. Lydia's grave eyes brightened; by that swift act, Della had belied the gruff callousness of her reply.

"Don't fuss so, Della. I'm fine," Letitia Burnan indignantly protested as the registered nurse took a small round pillow and eased it behind her mistress's shoulders. "Land sakes, seems to me if you want my money so bad, you wouldn't work so hard to keep me alive."

"That's my training coming out, Mrs. Burnan." Della

chuckled as she drew up a straight-backed chair for Lydia. "Once you've become a nurse, you automatically work at keeping folks alive, even if they're just about the meanest possible, present company not excepted."

Lydia caught her breath at this rude riposte. Letitia Burnan heard the faint gasp, and leaned forward, a placating smile on her thin pale lips. "You musn't take any notice of the two of us, my dear," her voice was gentler now. "We'd neither of us be happy unless we were insulting each other—isn't that right, Della?"

"We get along, I guess," Della's tone was grudging. "That's because I'm on to all your tricks by now. But you didn't have Lydia come here this morning to hear our wrangling. Better have her start in reading for you, right?"

"What would you like me to read to you today, Mrs. Burnan?" Lydia interposed.

"You know, I feel in the mood for some poetry. Do you like poetry, Lydia?" Letitia Burnan's sightless eyes fixed on Lydia and the young brunette had the uncanny feeling that she could actually see, so unwavering was her look.

"Yes, I do, very much," Lydia eagerly proffered. "My father used to write it."

Then she bit her lips, abashed at her own temerity. Not once during any of her previous visits to the Burnan house had she ever volunteered anything about her own background. The very first day, Mrs. Burnan had asked her about her schooling and her future plans; and Lydia had told her simply that both her parents were dead, that she lived with her Aunt Corinne, and that she had gone to high school here in New York, spent a year out of school accompanying her aunt on a European trip, and then completed a year of study and training so that she could obtain her license as a practical nurse. And Mrs. Burnan had never tried to pry out of her any other information about her own past. Their reading sessions

41

had always been highly enjoyable, because from time to time Mrs. Burnan would wave to Lydia to stop for a moment while she dwelt on some reminiscence which the passage that Lydia had just read had evoked in her still keen and colorful mind. There were also times when Mrs. Burnan would ask Lydia about her own views concerning something the girl was reading to her. It was always stimulating and thought-provoking to spend the morning in this huge library with its neatly ordered bookcases around three walls.

The wall opposite the door was marked in the middle by a mock fireplace and just above the richly lustered mahogany mantelpiece there hung a small framed oil painting. It was an abstract scene entitled "Manhattan Snows;" it had been painted by Mrs. Burnan's son Charles. Lydia had often visited the Museum of Modern Art, and she was frank to admit that she was not a modernist at heart so far as painting was concerned. It was Della who had told her the identity of the painter, as well as a good many things about Charles Burnan which Lydia was certain should never have been discussed with a stranger. That was how she knew about Charles's three divorces and his mercurial inability to hold any kind of prosaic job.

There must have been at least two thousand books in the library, Lydia estimated. They had never actually been catalogued, but Della had put Lydia's predecessors to work every now and then arranging them into groups of fiction, nonfiction, and biography. The bookcase which flanked the doorway to the library, which was on the east wall, contained mainly biographies and books on travel. The opposite wall, divided by the mock fireplace, housed books on science, economics, the fine arts, and poetry. There were many magnificently printed Skira art books in those cases, books which Mrs. Burnan had bought for Charles, which he had leafed through perhaps once or twice and then never looked at again. And the south wall, broken only by an old cherry wood secretary at the farthest corner, afforded space for five large wide bookcases, all of which were packed with novels and volumes of short stories. A good many of these, indeed, dated back to Letitia Burnan's own days as a schoolteacher, and many of them had nearly fallen apart from constant use. Sometimes, after Lydia had finished reading, Mrs. Burnan would ask her to get one of those old books and hand it to her. Then the blind old woman would smile and carefully open the volume, her long wrinkled fingers brushing over the tops of the pages as if searching for corners that she had turned down perhaps sixty years before. When that happened, Della would make a sign to Lydia that she was to go out quietly and come back on the next morning scheduled for her visit. And Della would go out, quietly closing the library door behind her, leaving Edward Burnan's widow alone with the brightly kindled memories of her young womanhood.

Letitia Burnan seemed to lean forward a little more intently in her wheelchair and her sear features came alive with the same animation she had shown when she was imbuing her fifth grade students with an enthusiasm for the three "R's." "I didn't know that your father was a writer, Lydia dear. Did he ever have anything published?"

Lydia flushed and nervously twisted her slim fingers in her lap. She hadn't meant to let anything slip out about her father. Now that she had, it only served to remind her more acutely and painfully that she had never actually read anything that he had written. Except for one of his poems, which she had found on a typed sheet of foolscap lying on the floor of the attic near the grandfather's clock just a few days before her mother's death. She'd read it and she hadn't quite understood what it meant, except that it seemed to tell a story. She had folded it up and put it into the pocket of her dress and gone on

43

playing. She had meant to give it back to him, but he had stayed down at the paper late that night to get out three or four of his special columns done in advance so that he and her mother could take a short vacation in San Francisco.

The next morning, Lydia had gone out to play with Beckie and Gloria and she had forgotten all about the poem which she had put into her prayer book. She had always gone to church with her parents and she had liked Dr. Wilson's sermons. Her father had liked them, too. He used to tell her that religion could never work if you had to scare people into it by preaching hell-fire and brimstone all the time. And Dr. Wilson never did that.

That poem . . . at her mother's funeral, she had remembered it while Dr. Wilson was talking at the grave-side. Because it had been about death, too, but her father had been so stunned by her mother's death that she'd decided it wouldn't be a good idea to give him back the poem because it might only remind him of everything that had happened. So she'd kept it in the prayer book. The little prayer book with the faded black cover and the gold lettering, "My Prayer Book." Why, now she remembered—she still had it. When Aunt Corinne had taken her on the train to New York, she had carried it with her. She hadn't had much chance to read it, though, because Aunt Corinne kept talking all the way through the trip about the wonderful opportunities she, Lydia, would have from now on and how hard Aunt Corinne was going to try to be a mother to her. And the prayer book was in her dresser drawer under the handkerchiefs. It was strange that she couldn't remember seeing the folded piece of foolscap. Perhaps it had fallen out years ago. . . .

"Yes, Mrs. Burnan, he worked on a newspaper back in a small town in California. He wrote lots of articles and columns." Purposely, she was noncommittal. After all, Mrs. Burnan paid her to read books aloud, not to talk about her own life.

But the blind woman's alert face indicated that she had no intention of letting this absorbing new topic be terminated quite so quickly. "No, no, my dear," she pursued, "I mean, did he ever have a book of his poetry or articles or, maybe, stories printed?"

Lydia looked up and saw Della standing near the wheelchair regarding her with a stern expression. The registered nurse brusquely nodded, made a peremptory gesture with her hand as much as to say, "Go ahead."

"Well, yes, he did have one book published. It was a novel. And some short stories in national magazines," Lydia hesitantly replied.

"A novel, you say, my dear? What was the title?"

"It was called *No Lost Arrears*."

Letitia Burnan turned her face towards the window, and the sun's rays dappled her forehead, wrinkling now in concentration. "Why, that's very familiar . . . that's out of one of Edwin Arlington Robinson's poems . . . I'm sure I remember what it is . . . yes, I have it now— it's from the poem, 'Vickery's Mountain.' Lydia, there's a dear girl, see if you can find it for me in his *Collected Poems*. I'm sure you can find it in that bookcase that contains most of my poetry books."

"Yes, Mrs. Burnan." Lydia had begun to tremble. The blind woman's startlingly acute recollection had suddenly lighted a flame where before there had been only obscure darkness. She walked quickly to the bookcase and began to scan the titles, her eyes wide and anxious. The book was the very first at the left on the third shelf; its red cloth cover had gold lettering with the poet's signature reproduced on the front. "H-here it is," she exclaimed, and took it out, clutching it with both hands to her bosom, for her heart had begun to pound with a frightening urgency.

"Look in the front at the table of contents, under the title of 'Vickery's Mountain,'" Letitia Burnan urged. She smiled and leaned back in her wheelchair with a sigh of pleasure as if she had solved a knotty problem.

Lydia turned the first few pages, her gaze sweeping down each in search of the title. At last she exclaimed, "I've found it, Mrs. Burnan! It's right after 'Miniver Cheevy' on page 349."

"You see, Della?" Letitia turned her smiling face toward where the registered nurse was standing. "Maybe I'm ready for the boneyard, but I'm still not in my dotage." Then, impatiently, to Lydia: "Did you find that phrase yet, dear?"

Lydia, carefully perusing the page, her slim forefinger moving down the stanzas, nodded. Then she read aloud:

> Since then a crafty score of years
> Have come, and they have gone;
> But Vickery counts no lost arrears;
> He lingers and lives on.*

"That's it, that's it!" Letitia Burnan jubilantly crowed. It's one of Robinson's minor efforts, but, like everything he wrote, there's a juicy kernel in there for the person with a smart mind to chew on." Then, her moment of triumph quite forgotten, she urged, her voice strangely gentle, "Do tell me more about your father, my dear. He must have been a very remarkable man. And he must have loved Robinson's poetry as much as I do."

"He-he did, Mrs. Burnan." Lydia glanced down at the thick book she held in her hands. "He died before I came to New York to live with my Aunt Corinne. He died right after my mother did."

* Edwin Arlington Robinson, "Vickery's Mountain," *The Town Down the River*, New York, Charles Scribner's Sons, 1910. *Collected Poems of Edwin Arlington Robinson*, The Macmillan Company, New York, 1935.

"Oh, you poor child!" Letitia Burnan compassionately shook her head. "I didn't know—I'm sorry, dear, and I didn't mean to pry."

"It—it's all right, Mrs. Burnan." Lydia looked down again at the stanza she had just read aloud. "Of course, I miss him very much, and Mother too, even after all these years. And I'm sorry that I never got a chance to read Father's book. He and Mother always said I was too young. There used to be a copy in our library, but when we moved out here to New York, it wasn't there any more."

The blind old woman tilted back her head, her sightless eyes staring up at the ceiling, her forehead once again furrowed as she imperiously sought to summon back a long mislaid article from her crowded storeroom of memories. Half aloud, she repeated the title of Arthur Turner's book, than rapped on the arm of her wheelchair with her bony knuckles. "Yes, of course, that's why I remembered the poem—It's because I've read your father's book. In fact, I'm sure I have it. Lydia, darling, go look over in the big bookcases with all the fiction, and see if you can't find it. I just know I've read it, and I never throw away a book I like."

Once again, as when she had smiled back at the little girl in *L'Armorique*, Lydia's face brightened into beauty as she hurried over to the wall with the five large bookcases and the cherry wood secretary. Della Hargell watched her move in turn from bookcase to bookcase, first standing in front of each with her head turning from left to right as she scanned the titles, then stooping so that she could see the books on the lower shelves. Meanwhile, Letitia Burnan impatiently turned her chair about in the direction of that wall, trying by the very intensity of her will power to aid the young brunette in her search.

"I do wish I could remember just exactly where it is, dear," she called. "It's not a very thick book, I seem to

47

remember, and I think it has a green cloth cover. Della, don't just stand there gawking as I know you're doing. Go over and help Lydia find it."

"Yes ma'am." Della rolled her eyes and emitted an exasperated sigh, the latter for Mrs. Burnan's benefit. But she at once walked over to the very last case on the right and began to look. And it was she, indeed, who found the book on the next to last shelf, in between a copy of *The Young Lions* and *The Hickory Stick*.

"I've got it!" Della called out as she straightened, holding the book aloft. "And it doesn't have a green cloth cover, either. It's more a powder blue, so you see, Mrs. Burnan, your memory's not as good as you think it is!"

She handed the book to Lydia with a wink and a faint smile that told the girl this latest abusive comment on her employer's faculties was merely part of the unending game she played. And Lydia, smiling back, her eyes misting with sudden tears, understood.

"You've found it? Good! Lydia, dear, by all means take it home with you and read it. For that matter, since I'm sure it would be hard for you to find another copy, why don't you keep it? I think I know how very much it means to you." And then, to forestall the brunette's tremulous thanks, Mrs. Burnan added, "No, no, don't thank me, my dear. Now, won't you read to me from Robinson? I think I'd like to start with his 'The Man Who Died Twice.' "

Chapter Six

It was not until midafternoon that Lydia returned from the old brownstone house in the Bronx. As was her wont, Aunt Corinne was taking a nap in her bedroom with the door closed. She had told Lydia just before the young brunette had left for Mrs. Burnan's to wake her no later than four o'clock if she were still sleeping; this evening they were going to Mercurio's for a real Italian dinner of *Rogoncino Trifolate* (veal kidneys cooked with mushrooms, truffles, and sherry) and, for dessert, one of those heavenly *Cassata con Fragoles* and a bottle of that cool clear Orvieto which never left you with a sour stomach the next morning even if you drank the whole bottle. After that they were going to see Bea Lillie in "Blithe Spirit."

It was almost three o'clock, but that left Lydia a full hour. She went directly to her room, which was the smallest in the entire apartment, even smaller than the kitchen. There was a big lavishly furnished living room with ceiling-high windows looking out on Park Avenue; Aunt Corinne's bedroom and huge private bathroom with sunken tub, all done in black marble and green tile; the kitchen, Lydia's own room and bathroom, and a sort of breakfast nook-dinette which connected with the living room through an archway and was large enough to use whenever Aunt Corinne wanted to give a dinner party for six or eight guests.

Lydia had wanted to bring her old dresser along, because her mother had bought it for her on her seventh birthday . . . not the day before Christmas, but on

June 12, which her mother had laughingly told her would be her very special secret birthday so that she could get extra presents. It had three wide drawers and two small ones at the top, and a round mirror in a very attractive frame of knotty pine. Aunt Corinne had moved only a few of the pieces of furniture from the house in Trubecke to the Park Avenue apartment, but she had finally relented and allowed Lydia to bring her dresser. The room was small and had a single window which looked down into the courtyard of the building. Its closet was small, too, but then Lydia didn't need a large closet, since her wardrobe hardly approached the proportions of Aunt Corinne's.

Lydia had, at most, four dresses, two of them for dining out and going to the theater; a plain cloth coat which was sturdy enough for New York winters, and a lighter coat for spring and early summer. She had three pairs of shoes; two of them already with the heels worn down. She had worn them during her year at the hospital getting her practical nurse's license, and she had been on her feet constantly. She would never have been able to wear Aunt Corinne's high-fashion skyscraper heeled pumps. And she really didn't care much for fancy clothes, even if she did stop once in a while to look at the temptingly arranged displays in the windows along Park and Fifth Avenues.

The plain white uniform of a nurse was utilitarian and comfortable, and it had nothing to do with style or showing off; it was a symbol. When you wore it, people knew that your job was to help the sick and the old and the very young who were crippled or retarded or in pain, just as you recognized that symbol when others wore it going to and from the hospitals all over New York, wearing coats in bad weather over plain white uniforms, with the white stockings and the low-heeled shoes. You knew that they were on their way to help people who needed them; it was a good feeling to know that you belonged in that circle. Because it was neither a clique nor a socially predicated sorority; everyone who wore a nurse's uniform had made some sort of sacrifice, endured some kind of privation, preferred the long hours and the grueling, often thankless, work of caring for people who could not care for themselves.

Lydia knew very well how limited her opportunities would be as a practical nurse, but even so, she was grateful for having been able to do something . . . like reading to those children in the ward. That was why she admired Della Hargell so much and was beginning, at last, to understand that Della's gruffness and bullying was perhaps a mask that hid deep welling sympathy and concern. Some day, if this job with Mrs. Burnan went on long enough and she was able to save her money, Lydia might be able to continue her studies and become a registered nurse like Della. Then she wouldn't have just one relative—Aunt Corinne; she would have many people of all ages and kinds who looked to her for help and allowed her to take joy in giving that help.

Besides the dresser, the girl's room was furnished with a narrow bed and a modern, but not too comfortable, armchair as well as a little night table beside the bed with a lamp which she often used for reading. Whenever she could, she took books from the library and studied them. Books about medicine and nursing, so that if she ever got the chance, she wouldn't find it too hard to keep up with the classes. If she wanted to be a registered nurse, she really ought to be in school right now, because in seven more months she would be twenty-one years old; and, even if she started her advanced studies now, it would take at least another three years before she could hope to get her rating as an R.N.

There was a maid service in the apartment building, and the Negro girl came in twice a week. But Aunt

Corinne was so fussy that Lydia herself, without being told, mopped and dusted whenever she thought it was necessary.

Laying her father's novel down on top of the dresser, Lydia opened the left-hand top drawer and put her hand under the pile of plain cotton handkerchiefs. Yes, her little prayer book was there. She took it out and leafed through it. But the folded sheet of foolscap with her father's poem wasn't inside the book at all. Perhaps it had fallen out of the book years ago. So much had happened since she had left the house in Trubecke. Still, she ought to have been more careful. Until this afternoon, it had been her only memento of her father's writing. Of course, the novel would be even better. Just the same, Lydia was sorry she had lost the poem.

She had really nothing left of Father except her memories. Not even a picture. There had been a large framed picture in the living room back in the house at Trubecke. She had naturally assumed that Aunt Corinne had packed it with the other things that would be taken to New York. But, when she had helped Aunt Corinne unpack the trunks and the furniture crates that had been sent on by truck, the picture wasn't there at all. And Aunt Corinne had let out a sigh, shaken her head, and said, "Oh, you poor darling—what with the way I was so upset about what happened to my poor sister and then your father, I must have left it back in some of those boxes which we decided to store up in the attic. You will forgive me, won't you?"

She put the prayer book back under the pile of handkerchiefs and closed the drawer. Then she took the book from the dresser and went back to the armchair, sat down, and opened it. Again, Lydia felt her eyes blur with tears. She blinked them impatiently, angry with herself. She thought that she had learned enough self-control by this time. That was part of her training as a nurse; you might care very deeply for an individual patient, yet you must never show favoritism or sorrow, or anything that would tend to lessen the patient's trust in you. It was such a kind of blind dependent trust— like a little child with his arm in a cast looking up at you with big pain-darkened eyes and saying, "It hurts, it hurts! Can't you stop it hurting me?" And if you broke down and cried, then the child would think that you were helpless when you really weren't. No, she hadn't at all meant to let Mrs. Burnan know about her father. Because even that kind generous old woman would be wanting to talk about her father again, the very next time she went, and that would only remind Lydia of what she had been trying to forget. For he had gone so abruptly from her, and she had been denied even the final parting at his funeral, when she could have cried and shown her grief in front of everyone without being ashamed of it, because she had loved him so.

But there had been no funeral. She knew only that Aunt Corinne had told her that he had died. And that news, following so closely upon the terrible death of her mother, had shocked her into an unthinking, unquestioning state. It was only when she and her aunt were on the train for New York that she had thought to ask Aunt Corinne how he had died. And Aunt Corinne had said, putting an arm about her shoulders and speaking very gently, "My poor darling, I didn't want to tell you everything because it was so morbid. Maybe it's better that you don't know, that you have to accept only that you won't see him again."

But when Lydia had insisted on knowing, Aunt Corinne had said, "He must have been beside himself with grief over your mother, Lydia, darling. Because he drove away in his old Plymouth and went out on Route 99, up the mountains from Bakersfield towards Los Angeles, and his car crashed into one of the ravines. It was at night, and I think he had been drinking to forget about your mother. Now, you mustn't remember that, you must remember Arthur just as he was, and we'll say no more about it."

If Lydia closed her eyes now, she could begin to remember what he looked like—the way she had seen him smiling at Mother in the library; the book that they had both been reading aloud by turn fallen to the floor unnoticed, while they held hands and looked at each other with such joy. Now, she couldn't see the print on the pages of the book she had just opened, not until she dried her eyes and blew her nose and told herself that Father wouldn't have wanted her to act this way at all.

Lydia opened the book to the title page. It read: "*No Lost Arrears* by Arthur Turner." Then, at the bottom: "Hargood-Rawson. New York, 1950." Lydia didn't recognize the publisher's name, although by now she knew most of the big houses in New York, like Doubleday, Random House, and Simon & Schuster. Maybe it had never been a big success nor a lot of copies been sold, but Father had written it and Mother had said to her that it was a kind of love story. Maybe reading it now would take her back to the time when she was six years old, which had been the happiest time of all for her, because it was during that year that her father had been made assistant editor of the paper in Trubecke and had had this book printed by the New York publisher, even though he was a writer in a small California town that very few people across the country had heard about.

Then Lydia was held spellbound, and the view of the courtyard and of the New York skyline fell away, and she was back in Trubecke, back in the attic which had given her so many hours of happiness, of fantasy, and illusion.

No Lost Arrears was not a long book, about three hundred pages in all, but Lydia dwelt over every paragraph. Though trained to read quickly in high school and at the hospital, Lydia abandoned the swift photographic method she had used for cramming facts as speedily as

54

possible into her assimilating mind, and found herself mulling over the words, the phrases, just as Aunt Corinne would delectate over a glass of vintage Haut Brion.

For the book was a kind of allegory, charmingly and heartwarmingly written; her mother had been right in calling it a love story, for there, for those to see who had known her parents' nature and essential goodness of heart, was their own story set forth.

Arthur Turner had pictured himself as a hesitant and would-be knight, without spear or armor won in battle, no Sir Gawaine or Brian the Bull, but a timid scrivener who, having been squire in a lordly mansion, fell ill and dreamed. And his dreams foreshadowed a beautiful lady far away in the Kingdom of the West, who would one day give him her gage and knight him with her accolade, though others might laugh and call him no worthy shield bearer, but a cowardly upstart who sought by dint of stealth and trickery to win the prize so unattainable—a prize which worthier, more gallant men had long coveted. And, then, after recovering from his illness, the scrivener had set forth on his lonely journey to that Kingdom of the West, inwardly dreading the dragons and the giants and the ogres who beset his way. But Fortune had smiled on him and lighted his way and kept it clear of the pitiless foes who would have barred his path to his lady.

The lady was guarded by a jealous duenna, who tested the squire and sorely tried him before she permitted her gentle mistress to exchange words with him. And there was also a suitor, a bold young knight, not of noble birth, but of lowly heritage, who sneered at him and told him that he could never win the lady. But win her he had, and he had settled down with her in the Kingdom of the West, and taken up pen instead of lance to slay the dragons of bigotry, spitefulness, and envy that were deadlier by far than those which breathed forth fire and smoke, because these other dragons were invisible, yet all around. And the sun had shown on him and his lady, and he had been blessed with a daughter as lovely and as gentle as her mother, and so he feared no longer any dragons. And he had no lost arrears, no debts from the past to pay. Only those which the future might hold, and, to meet them, he felt himself heroically endowed.

There was wit, charm, and wistfulness in her father's writing, and Lydia, absorbed in the allegory, figuring for herself the identity of each of those characters who seemed so distant and yet so curiously alive, forgot the time. It was not till she put down the book and glanced at her inexpensive little wrist watch that she realized she had quite forgotten to wake Aunt Corinne and that it was quarter of six.

Horrified, she rose from the chair and was about to open the door and go to her aunt's bedroom when it was suddenly flung open and Aunt Corinne, in a green satin negligee and mules, her face puffy with sleep and her eyes angrily narrowed, shrilled: "Do you know what time it is, Lydia? You let me sleep—now, we'll be late to dinner and never make the show! You thoughtless, ungrateful girl—I ask so little of you after all I've done, yet there you stay in your room without a thought for me. What were you doing, after you came back from Mrs. Burnan's, that you couldn't remember to wake me at four as you were told?"

"I—I'm terribly sorry, Aunt Corinne," Lydia faltered, "I really was going to wake you just as you told me. But Mrs. Burnan——" She stopped, suddenly aware that the admission she was about to make would only infuriate her aunt the more. To confess having read a book and, consequently, to have forgotten a prescribed duty would be like throwing oil on a bonfire.

But before Lydia could compose her mind and rearrange her words to give some satisfactory explanation,

Aunt Corinne saw the blue-cloth-bound book which Lydia had laid on the dresser. Her eyes narrowed, and her lips tightened with a vindictive meanness.

"Where did you get that book?" Aunt Corinne demanded, her voice shrilly raw with rancor and suspicion.

"Mrs. Burnan gave it to me. She had it in her library, and——"

Arms akimbo, forehead creased with annoyance, Corinne Edwards contemptuously declared: "I suppose you had to go blabbing to that senile creature all about your family problems. Do you think she's interested in you?"

"I didn't discuss anything that happened back in Trubecke, Aunt Corinne," Lydia protested, with cheeks reddening from the brusk, undeserved reprimand. "She wanted me to read some of Robinson's poetry to her and she asked me if I knew his work. I said that my father had loved his poetry and that he used to write poetry himself. Then she asked me if Father had written anything else, and I told her about his novel. It just happened that she had the book in her library. She has thousands of books in that big room. Besides, I don't see that I did any harm at all, and I've a right to be proud of my father for what he did."

Her aunt emitted a bitter little laugh. "Oh, yes, very proud, indeed, I'm sure! When everybody in Trubecke is still saying that your father killed your mother and——"

"Stop it! Don't ever say such a horrible thing again. Do you hear, Aunt Corinne?" Lydia cried, beside herself. "You know very well that he was acquitted at the trial. And he had no reason to kill my mother—he loved her, just as he loved me. Yes, I read his book just now, and that's why I forgot to wake you up, because I'd never read any fiction he wrote before—it was so

57

wonderful that I forgot all about the time. I'm sorry I didn't wake you up, Aunt Corinne. But you mustn't ever say dreadful things about my father again. He was a good man, and he didn't hate anybody—he just couldn't—it wasn't in him to hate. Maybe I was just a little girl when it all happened, but I know how good he was."

Aunt Corinne passed a hand over her forehead, closed her eyes, uttered a groan. "Please, Lydia—all right, I'm sorry if I hurt your feelings. But do you realize what time it is, girl? Now, don't upset me any more with your silly talk. Hurry and get yourself ready for dinner. As it is, we're hardly going to have time to eat if we expect to see Bea Lillie."

"If it's all the same to you, Aunt Corinne, I'd just as soon not go. Thank you very much anyway." Lydia's voice was choked by tears.

Her aunt shrugged. "Suit yourself, then, Lydia. There —now, I've got a headache, and it's all your fault. Oh, dear. Well I suppose I'd better hurry if I'm going to go by myself. That's the thanks I get for looking after you."

On the threshold, she turned and looked back, her sensual mouth scornfully curled. "I shouldn't have said what I did about your father, perhaps, Lydia. But I'll tell you this much—you say he didn't have it in him to hate. I say he did. That trashy book of his you've been reading is full of it. Who was he anyway? A nobody from Chicago—who came to Trubecke to marry my sister who could have had her pick of wealthy young men from all over the state. Arthur set himself up as better than the people in the town where he was earning his living. A writer, yes, and writers are a dime a dozen. But he was lucky. He married your mother, and he stood to inherit the Edwards fortune under the California community property law. If you want to know something, Lydia, I destroyed that book before we left for New York. I never wanted you to read it. And you'd do better, for your own peace of mind and your own good, to forget all about your father."

Then she was gone. Lydia sank down into the armchair, covered her burning face with her hands and wept.

Chapter Seven

IT WAS as if all the tears that Lydia had held back during these past eight years had suddenly been released from the inner reservoir which she had striven to dam against the crumbling betrayal of emotion. She wept, but not for herself nor for the insolent contempt with which Aunt Corinne had treated her all this while. Her tears were for her father, maligned without the opportunity for self-defense. For even her love could not redeem his name now. If what Aunt Corinne had said was true—that the people back in Trubecke still thought of him only as the Midwestern upstart who had come there without invitation to marry into the most illustrious family of the town and that very likely he had found some clever way of getting rid of his bride without paying the penalty demanded by law—then not even her unswerving faith in him could eradicate such bigotry. And even if she went back there now to champion his name, what could she accomplish? They would say: "It's natural that a twelve-year-old child should love her father, but what could she know at that age about what he did and what he was?"

Yes, he had been acquitted by a jury of his peers of the charge of murdering her mother. But, even now, just as during that trial, there were those from Trubecke who believed him guilty, who wanted to believe him guilty, because they distrusted him as an "outsider." And that damning judgment would never be amended, once it had been rendered. She remembered how Beckie had rejected her, in a way that decreed that

60

she was as guilty as her father simply because she was his own flesh and blood. After all these years, what tangible proof could she find to prove their judgments wrong and spiteful? And yet she would go on to her dying day obsidian-firm in her inner knowledge that Father could never have committed such a crime.

But then, who had? How was it that her mother's car had been tampered with and to what purpose? Why had her father vanished without even having left a note for her or a message with Dolores? After her father's death —what could Dolores have told her about the mystery of her mother's death and then of her father's strange disappearance? A week or two after Aunt Corinne had announced to Lydia the news of his death, Dolores had left the old house to go back to her kinfolk in Guadalajara. One of her sisters had been very ill and she was going to stay with her for awhile and then, perhaps, come back to enter domestic service with another family. That was what her aunt had told Lydia. She hadn't mentioned Inez, but Lydia had assumed that Inez, being Dolores's niece, would naturally accompany her back to Mexico.

But at least this day, which had brought her aunt's resentment and condescension out into the open, had had its compensation for all these prior years of loneliness— she had something of her father's which she could cherish. For, into this book, regardless of its commercial success or failure, he had put his thoughts, the quintessence of his hopes and ambitions, and his love for both her mother and herself. And that was something neither Aunt Corinne nor the entire town of Trubecke with its hostile, clannish verdict against her father, could ever take away from her.

It had been like a miracle, she thought, that Mrs. Burnan should have had her father's book in that vast, expensive library. So many, many books were written and published every year, so many of them forgot-

61

ten, gathering dust on library shelves or jumbled in the outside bin of a second-hand book store. Yet here, thousands of miles across the country, before she had gone blind, an old woman who had let neither wealth nor age stifle her love for life, had bought her father's book and read it and kept it fourteen years after its publication. A woman whom she respected and admired had shared and understood her father's message, thought him sensitive and imaginative. And this perhaps was a greater vindication of her father than Lydia could ever hope to achieve by herself back in Trubecke.

She was exhausted from her fit of crying. And yet she felt relief from it even through the fatigue. Aunt Corinne had not seen those tears; she would not have the satisfaction of knowing how cruelly her sneering words about Lydia's father had lashed the girl. And Aunt Corinne would remember that Lydia had delivered an ultimatum: she would accept this bread of charity and this subservience; she would acquiesce to the petty little impositions and the menial errands and the penance of listening to her aunt's selfish prattling of all her gourmandizing and touring and display of possessions; but only in return for Aunt Corinne's saying no more denigrating things about her father.

Yet with that ultimatum, Lydia sensed that henceforth her own position in this household would be strained and cheerless. If she only had enough money to continue her schooling as a nurse! But even a steady year of employment with Mrs. Burnan, three mornings a week at thirty-five dollars per week would not give her the money she needed for that schooling. And she would never again accept a loan from Aunt Corinne. Perhaps she should be more practical now and ask for an accounting; certainly, just as Aunt Corinne had mentioned, under the California community property law, there had been some money left to her by her parents. Had it truly been entirely expended?

Legally, she would come of age at twenty-one. Perhaps she should have found herself a clerical job and tried to survive as best she could by herself and without dependence on Aunt Corinne. Yet the ties of blood were strong; how many times she had told herself, after one of Aunt Corinne's typical scenes at a restaurant or night club, that Aunt Corinne was her mother's sister and the only remaining link between her and her dead parents. There was no one else to claim her. And, of course, as a child, she could not have broken away even if she had wanted to. They would either have returned her to Aunt Corinne or put her in some kind of institution. By passive acceptance, she had at least obtained her schooling as a practical nurse. And she had Aunt Corinne to thank for that. One balanced and one compromised with life as best one could.

Lydia rose from the armchair, glancing at her wristwatch. It was a little past seven o'clock. By this time, Aunt Corinne had certainly left. For an instant, a wry smile touched Lydia's soft, tear-humid lips. She could already imagine Aunt Corinne's frenetic impatience at Mercurio's at this very moment, urging all and sundry to hurry the preparation of her dinner so that she wouldn't miss the theater, yet at the same time insisting that everything be perfection itself. It was a poor joke, but it sufficed to distract Lydia from the bitter recollections which her aunt had evoked.

It was high time that she thought of her own supper, too. Della had brought Mrs. Burnan and her their lunch at noon, and then Lydia had gone on reading poetry for several hours. From time to time, Mrs. Burnan had stopped her, either to ask her to repeat a particularly pleasing line or to comment on what it meant especially to her. And, for Lydia herself, the choice of reading matter had been a dual inspiration: not only because the works of Robinson had been dear to her father but also because, encountering them really for the first time herself, she had felt some of that same excitement which a listener to music may experience on hearing a great symphony for the first time. While she had read aloud, exquisite thrills of pleasure had run through her as she came upon a delicately complex metaphor or a vivid phrase which, at a single stroke, served to underline a person or a situation which Robinson was describing.

When at last Letitia Burnan had leaned back in her wheelchair and given a little nod to signify that she had listened enough for the day, Lydia had thanked her for the copy of her father's book. Since the beginning of that session, Mrs. Burnan had asked no more questions about her father. But when Lydia was ready to leave, the blind woman had asked her to come the very next day, instead of waiting until two days later, as had been the custom. Usually Lydia came either Mondays, Wednesdays, and Fridays, or Tuesdays, Thursdays, and Saturdays.

Part of the fatigue she now felt, relaxed though it was after this unusual excess of weeping—so unlike her usual behavior—was due to the demanding spiritual impact which Robinson's poetry had made on her. She knew nothing of the poet's life except that her father had once mentioned that Theodore Roosevelt had given Robinson a job in the post office as a provisional subsidy which might help free his creative spirit from having to cope with the mundane problem of earning a livelihood.

But, as she had read Robinson's lines aloud to Mrs. Burnan, Lydia had perceived a kinship between the poet and her father: both of them strove eternally to find the "Light," which was Robinson's infallible symbol for the truth. To find the truth, cost what it might, had been the poet's credo. And it might well have been her father's too. Yet, at the very end, what hidden truth had he sought that had brought him to his death—or had his search really been the cause? Knowing how much he had loved her mother, Lydia, drawing upon her own practical knowledge of shock, pain, and suffering from her scant year as a nurse, had had to give grudging credence to Aunt Corinne's theory that grief had driven her father to take his own life. There was even a curious kind of similarity in the deaths of her father and her mother to substantiate that theory—her mother had died at the wheel of a car; so her father, distraught because of the loss of the woman he had so deeply loved, had tried to follow her even to the exactitude of a similar death.

Yet she would never really know. No matter what conjecture she contrived from the sparse facts she knew, it would remain conjecture and nothing more, and would grow dimmer and more unreal as time broadened the gulf between then and now.

To grapple with conjecture was to battle against ghosts. There could be no victory in this, for they were too tenuous to cling to, and it was impossible to hold them fast, if only for a fleeting moment so that even strangers could call them real. It was better to think of trivial things now which were real, such as her discovery that she was extremely hungry. By thinking thus, she forced her mind away from speculations that would only lead to brooding and despair.

But, first, she put her father's book away, in the first large drawer of her dresser, under her neatly ironed chaste white slips. She would read it again when the hurt had dulled and finally gone. Now, it was still too fresh and anguishing, too keenly haunting for her to force herself, as she must, to realize that nothing would bring her father back . . . and that by willing him back through the abandoned years of her existence far from the place of her birth, she would succeed only in making the immediate years ahead too disconsolate to endure.

Chapter Eight

EMPTY NOW except for herself, the lavishly furnished apartment had a kind of suspended unreality to it. It was very dark now, for the ominous rumbling of an imminent thunderstorm had turned the unruffled blue sky arched over Manhattan into a dirtied slate on which menacing black smudges swelled. Below and beyond, the kaleidoscopic merry-go-round of lighted buildings, neon signs, and automobile headlights danced before Lydia as she paused for a moment in the living room to look out at the city.

Here inside, all was silence, as if no one had ever lived here; yet the garish elegance of the overstuffed blue davenport, the thick green carpeting, and the tall ornate lamp with its huge hexagonal shade presupposed the existence of a pampered, important dweller. For a tiny moment, Lydia indulged herself in the fantasy of pretending that she lived here alone and that she had only to close the windows to shut out the oncoming storm and to be safe within this luxurious refuge. But then, as a pelting rain began to hurl itself against the windows towards the south end of the living room, Lydia dismissed these idle daydreams and hurried to pull the windows down. It reminded her of how she had sometimes played with Beckie and Gloria up in the attic in the old house in Trubecke on a summer afternoon and of how then, as now, without the least warning, a thunderstorm had launched itself upon the house—how all three of them had scrambled to the narrow oval windows and tugged them down with almost frantic zeal, as if the first big drops of slanting rain were invaders storming a castle wall which needs must be repelled.

There was a writing desk and a straight-backed chair in front of it in the left corner of the south end of the living room, very near one of the open windows. Indeed, its glowing, dark mahogany top was already damp, and Lydia hurriedly dried it with her own handkerchief. The desk was plainly anachronistic, clashing with the rest of the furniture in the spacious room, but it had belonged to Aunt Corinne's father, Jonathan Edwards. The drawer just under the top was as wide as the desk itself, and there were two sturdy drawers below it on each side. It was a comfortable old desk, and one could sit on the straight-backed chair and comfortably put one's knees under it without bumping them.

At the back of the desk, to the right and almost on the edge of the top, right up against the window, there stood a heavy antique silver candlestick, which had belonged to Aunt Corinne's mother. There was something under the candlestick now which looked like a folded piece of paper. As she closed the window, Lydia only vaguely noticed it. The room suddenly smelled musty. It was a pity to have to close the windows, for the air had been humid all afternoon and the driving rain outside had brought a welcome coolness. A sudden flash of lightning daggered the glowering sky, and almost instantly a savage clap of thunder followed it. Standing there in the dark, seeing the lights of the city blur into grotesque abstracts which a drunken painter might have daubed, Lydia felt her fatigue ebb. It was almost as if the storm were a palliative that cleansed and eased her.

Lydia felt excruciatingly hungry, though not for the rich fare that Aunt Corinne was probably bolting down at that very moment. A salad, perhaps, some crackers and cheese, and a glass of iced coffee—black and strong. Outside, the storm was still growling its warning to the timid to stay inside where they would be safe. She had never been afraid of the elements. In Trubecke, with its stretches of uninteresting, flat brownish green landscape broken only by the squat clusters of hills to the west, the thunder and the lightning had always been more terrifying, and, often, they had come without the anodyne of rain. After a day of oppressive heat, when the sun had relentlessly beaten down upon a scorched earth, there would be drifting clouds, then the muffled drums of thunder declaiming after the lightning flashes. But the rain clouds would veer towards the south—and, when a new day dawned in Trubecke, it would be as shimmeringly hot as the day before. Sometimes, there would be torrential rain too; then the lightning would launch its blinding fingers towards the isolated houses within its reach. Once a bolt had struck the weather vane, and the windows had rattled all over the house.

Lydia shivered at the vivid acuteness of that childhood memory, and, as she did so, a violent flash of lightning, striking very near the apartment building, turned the outdoors into an infernal panorama. The silver candlestick, perilously perched on the very edge of the desk, toppled to the floor. As Lydia stooped to retrieve it, she noticed once again the folded piece of paper which had been placed beneath it. Only a dull white corner had peeped out before; now, it lay revealed, neatly folded into a square. Wonderingly, she picked it up with her left hand as she set the candlestick back in place with her right. Almost unthinkingly, she thrust the piece of paper into the pocket of her dress. Then she went out into the kitchen to prepare her simple supper. . . .

Tomorrow, she must really go shopping. The refrigerator was almost empty, and that wouldn't please Aunt Corinne at all. She'd go first thing in the morning—no, she had to go to Mrs. Burnan's again. Well, she'd do some marketing after she finished there. There was a fancy grocery store on Sixty-Eighth Street, and

Aunt Corinne particularly liked the fruits and vegetables they offered, though they were dreadfully expensive. But, for tonight, there was enough food to make do. Half a head of lettuce, one good-sized tomato and a piece of not too dry green pepper in the vitalizer. Yes, quite enough to make an edible salad. Now for the olive oil and vinegar. . . .

The tarragon vinegar was very strong, and, as Lydia opened the bottle, its pungent aroma made her sneeze. She groped for a handkerchief, vigorously blew her nose, and, still holding her handkerchief to her nose, poured a small amount of the vinegar over the ingredients in the salad bowl. Then she screwed the cap back onto the bottle and replaced it in the cupboard. As she turned to go back into the dinette where she could eat her supper and enjoy the view, her foot scuffed against the paper which had fallen out of her pocket. She put the salad bowl down on the counter and stooped to pick up the folded square. Then, prompted by some inexplicable impulse, she unfolded it.

It was a piece of white foolscap, badly faded and creased. On it was typed a poem—in elite type. She read it half aloud.

BLACKBIRDS

A man was murdered in our town one day.
All asked themselves who could have wished to kill
Him, and time passed. Then Jones, who ran a dray
Hauling orders out from the lumber mill,
Complained of blackbirds flying in his face.
"They dart at me, then swerve and quickly fly
Upwards to strike again in the same place.
I wish they'd stop!" That was his constant cry.

We found Jones in his room, quite dead, of course.
A note that savored of mythology
Told us in full what was the fatal force:

We knew something of ornithology.
"Those blackbirds—Furies in their vengeful rage——"
And then we knew that Jones had been a sage.

The typing was faded, too, but still quite legible. The
"*p*'s" seemed shorter than usual because their vertical
line seemed to have been chopped off at the bottom. And
the loops of the "*e*'s" were blurred. There was no doubt
about it. This sheet of foolscap had been typed on her
father's old portable machine. There were new creases
and folds in the paper, but from the deeper soiled creases,
Lydia could tell that it was the same piece of paper that
she had folded and put in her prayer book eight years
before.

Chapter Nine

How HAD that sheet of foolscap come to be under the candlestick on Aunt Corinne's writing desk? Why hadn't her aunt given it back to her? And, since Aunt Corinne thought so little of her father's writing ability, why had she bothered to keep it at all after having found it? That is—*if* she had found it.

No, no, it wasn't right for Lydia to think that. Aunt Corinne had never given her any reason to be suspicious about anything. Maybe she was a nagger and a fuss-budget about superficial things like meals and clothes, but she'd always given her straight answers to questions about school and the nursing training.

Aunt Corinne had never really been warmly affectionate, not even when they'd all lived together back in Trubecke. But that wasn't out of the ordinary at all. Lots of people were like that—careful not to let their emotions show. Lydia was that way herself, she knew— that was because she knew that a nurse had to control herself with a tight rein so that she wouldn't allow emotion to overcome good judgment and sound reasoning. In a crisis, the emotional person either vacillated or made a rash decision, and that could be fatal for a patient. It was true she'd never seen Aunt Corinne kiss her mother or put her arms around her, but that, too, wasn't so unusual. Lots of brothers and sisters went through life without doing that, yet they were fond of one another.

But Aunt Corinne must have found the piece of paper and folded it up again—the newer creases showed that. How long ago had she found it? Lydia didn't remember having seen it for a long time, almost as long as it had been since she got on the train to come to New York to start a new life with her aunt. Had it been in the apartment all this time, stuck under that wide-based candlestick? No, because she'd dusted the desk almost every other day herself and she certainly would have seen it along before his.

It was strange. Strange that the poem should have been opened and folded up so many times. Lydia certainly hadn't done it. Slowly, she turned it over, and then her eyes widened with surprise. She had just caught sight of some writing in pencil, very light, still discernible. What did it say? It was in a handwriting she didn't at all recognize. Bold, irregular, like a man's. It wasn't Aunt Corinne's, she knew. She had seen too many samples not to recognize her aunt's flowery script with its broadly looping "*L*'s" and "*W*'s." It read:

> "He's either a visionary or a crack-pot. They're both dangerous."

Who was a visionary or a crackpot, and why was he dangerous, and who had said that someone was? Since Aunt Corinne hadn't written those words on the back of the sheet of foolscap but had still retained the paper here in the apartment, how was it possible for a man to have written that puzzling comment on the back? Of course, Lydia didn't remember, so far back, whether that writing had been on the paper when she'd found it in the attic. Just the same, it was very strange. Why hadn't Aunt Corinne told her when she'd found it and given it back to her?

And the writing hadn't been put on the back of the paper recently. At least, it looked as light and faded as the typing itself. Maybe she was wrong, but she had the impression it had been written years ago. And that was strange, too.

Perhaps she should ask Aunt Corinne. But not to-night. Aunt Corinne would be tired and fretful when she got back after the theater, having had to rush through dinner all on Lydia's account. And they'd had that argument about her father. It would only antagonize her aunt a good deal more to ask questions about a piece of paper with typing on one side and somebody else's handwriting on the other. It wasn't her father's writing either—Lydia knew that much, too.

What did the poem mean? It was in the style of Edwin Arlington Robinson, in a way. The meaning within a meaning, drawn from seemingly unrelated incidents. "A man was murdered in our town one day." What had her father meant? Had he just thought up the poem, or had he been reminded of something that had actually happened in Trubecke? Or perhaps it had been in Chicago, before he had come to the West Coast. "Jones, who ran a dray . . . from the lumber mill, . . ." She hadn't known any Jones family in Trubecke. And there wasn't a lumber mill there either. The closest thing to it had been a feed and farm supply store. And the man who——

A cold chill ran down her spine. The man who had owned that store had been found shot to death one January night, the year of her parents' death. Sheriff Hines had said that the store had been broken into and robbed, and that Mr. Jerrell—that had been the owner's name, not Jones—must have tried to stop the burglar and been shot. The burglar who'd done it never had been caught——

Wait a minute . . . it was coming back. Her mother had died in June. And the month before, the *Reporter* had had a front-page story about a suicide. A man had cut his wrists and let himself bleed to death. And he'd left a note stating that he had something on his con-science that wouldn't let him rest, and he had to pay for it; this was the easiest way. He'd been a farmer, and his wife had left him and gone to another state early that year. Lydia remembered, because her father had discussed the case at the supper table. And she and he had, somehow, got on the subject of good and evil; she had asked how people who did evil were always punished. And Father had said, "Not always as we know it, Lydia, darling. Not in the courts where a man is sent to prison for a crime. But very often in the prison of his own mind, he pays a more terrible price. That's why most of us try to keep from doing harm and evil, because even if we get away with it as far as society is concerned, we must still live with and within ourselves."

A note that savored of mythology
Told us in full what was the fatal force:
We knew something of ornithology.
"Those blackbirds—Furies in their vengeful rage——"
And then we know that Jones had been a sage.

What had her father meant by those lines? *The prison of his own mind . . .* yes, of course! That man who had committed suicide and left that note about his conscience had sought to escape that prison. Had that farmer been the burglar who had shot Mr. Jerrell? Yet, if that were true, how had her father known about it?

How strange it was that all these memories were coming back, like insidious serpents gliding, unseen and unheard, under the dead leaves which strewed a well-worn path where there had never been serpents before.

The poem and the book and the storm. The sunny day that had begun like any other day in Lydia's routine, brightened only by the foreknowledge that much of it was to be spent with Mrs. Burnan, and then her own unthinking mention of her father's writing. From all this, the deeper delving back into a life she thought to have put a finish to when she crossed the country, the delving of a blind old woman's persistent,

74

retentive mind which had led to the discovery of her father's book.

The book; then the poem, followed by the singular writing on the back of that poem. And then her own mind, venturing farther than it had ever gone before into those past years, once joyous, then darkened by trage- dies, to seek associations with that poem.

The storm. So much like the summer storms back in Trubecke. Now it was subsiding—the rain had stopped. Only a vague murmur, far to the south. No more lightning.

It was a calm night now, and she was alone. And there was silence in the apartment. With the windows closed, it was as if she had sealed in all the ghosts of the past, and they were receding into their dark corners, vanishing, but only so they might return another time and, again, without giving warning.

And in that sepulchral silence, there now came to Lydia's awareness the loud imperious jangle of the tele- phone.

Chapter Ten

THE TELEPHONE was in the little hallway between the living room and the dinette. It rang steadily; yet in the stillness of the large, thickly carpeted apartment its sound was not muffled. As Lydia walked towards it, the sound seemed to grow shrill, as with a deep urgency.

She picked up the French phone. It was probably Aunt Corinne—no, that wasn't likely. If her aunt had gone on to the theater, the show wouldn't be out yet. Unless, of course, she'd come out during intermission——

"Miss Edwards' residence," Lydia said, as was her custom. Aunt Corinne wanted her to answer that way. After all, it was her aunt's apartment and she, herself, hardly expected anyone to call, unless it might be Della Hargell changing an appointment for Mrs. Burnan.

But it wasn't her aunt or Della. It was a man's voice, hoarse, halting.

"Which Miss Edwards?"

"Why, Miss Corinne Edwards. That is, it's her apartment, and I'm answering for her."

"I didn't think you were Corinne. She's out, I suppose?"

"Wh—who are you? Can I take a message? Yes, she is out, and I don't expect her back till about midnight."

"I see." There was a pause, and she could hear the man's breathing. Mystified, Lydia pursued: "Would you like to leave your name and number so she can get you in the morning?"

"No—no, thank you. Are you her niece Lydia?"

"Why, yes I am. Won't you tell me who you are?"

Again, the pause and the sound of breathing. A sudden anxiety took hold of her. She repeated: "Please—can't I take a message? I don't recognize your voice."

Then she heard, incongruously, a dry chuckle and: "Good. That's very good. You're Lydia Turner, then, aren't you?"

More and more puzzled, the young brunette stammered, "Yes, I am. Can't you tell me who are you, sir? I—I'm sorry, but I can't place you. Do—do you know me from here in New York—maybe the hospital?"

"No. Not the hospital." Again a pause. "Do you remember your father, Lydia?"

She had not been prepared for such a question. Or perhaps the events of this unforgettable day had shaken her. For she uttered a stifled cry, took the receiver from her ear, and looked at it, as if it had suddenly been transformed into a living thing.

"Hello. Hello."

The voice was louder now, it came to Lydia even though the receiver wasn't at her ear. With a gasp, she held it up again, answering, "Please—I don't understand all this. Won't you please tell me your name? Do you—did you——know my father?"

"If your father was Arthur Turner, the writer, yes. I knew him better than most men, Lydia."

"Oh, please—if this is a joke, it—it's cruel!" she burst out.

"Cruel?"

"If—if you knew my father, you—you'd know he died eight years ago. And to call me like this, without saying who you are or what you want and to ask me if I remember him, is cruel and in the worst taste. You've no right——"

The hoarse voice cut through her almost tearfully indignant remonstration: "But he's not dead, Lydia."

"Wh—what did you say?"

Her fingers ached from the convulsively fierce grip of the phone, and again her heart begun to pound. She was imagining all this. She was overwrought from having discovered her father's book and——

"I said, your father isn't dead, Lydia."

"For God's sake, don't torture me this way! He is dead, I know he is. Aunt Corinne told me—he was driving his car in the mountains and——"

Again, the hoarse voice interrupted her: "Were you at his funeral, Lydia?"

She caught her breath and felt herself trembling so violently that she could hardly stand. "N-no," she whispered back, her eyes wide and haunted. "No." There had been no funeral for her father. Aunt Corinne had told her that arrangements had been made without her knowledge, because Father had been so badly burned and mangled that it would have been too horrible for her, what with the so recent shock of her mother's death.

"Then you don't actually know that he's dead, do you, Lydia?"

If only she had Mrs. Burnan's uncannily keen hearing, so that she could recognize that hoarse voice, which chose its words with maddening deliberation!

"If—if not being at a funeral means I don't know that he was actually buried—you're right. Please—I—I can't stand this—why won't you identify yourself? How do you know he isn't dead? Where are you from?" She pleaded.

"You must believe me, Lydia. And trust me. I wouldn't harm you. I'd never joke and hurt you, surely not about such a thing."

Again, she was trembling, her fingers clutching the phone to her ear so that she could glean every sound, every breath, every inflection of this unknown voice.

"Then—then——" She forced herself to go on. "Why haven't I seen him in these eight years since I came to New York? If he—if he's still alive, why hasn't he come

78

to me and told me? Oh, no, how can you expect me to believe you—you won't even tell me who you are or how you know what you're telling me—no, no, I'm not going to listen——"

"He wrote a novel once, didn't he, Lydia?" Again, that hoarse, halting voice broke through her feverish denials. And again she gasped, this time with terror. For, in this entire city, so far as she knew, only her Aunt Corinne and Mrs. Burnan and Della Hargell knew about the novel. Yet this stranger who would not identify himself knew about it, too.

Now, craftily, to put him to the test, she demanded, "Tell me the title. Then I'll believe you knew my father. If you can't, I'm going to hang up."

"No, don't do that, please, Lydia!" The voice quivered with anxiety. "I can tell you that. It was *No Lost Arrears*."

In the distance, beyond the safety of the closed-in apartment, a final clap of thunder hurled defiance at the mortals below. Lydia uttered a startled cry.

"Oh—that—that's right! Please—I can't bear this suspense any more. Why won't you tell me who you are and what you know about my father?"

"Let's say—I'm a very close friend of his. One you never met, Lydia. But I tell you in all truthfulness that he's not dead. His car crashed and he was in it, but he didn't die. He was sick—for many years. But he's still alive. And he's become well-known and rich, too. He's written a book that's selling all over the country, and the money is put away, all for you. When the time comes, it'll be yours, and you'll be free of your dependence on your aunt."

"I—it—it—it's hard for me to believe you. I want to —I loved him so. C-can't you give me any proof—or tell me where I can find him? And, if he's alive, why hasn't he come to see me?"

Lydia sobbed. Before she had gripped the phone

in a frightened, angry defense against this macabre jest; now, she clutched it fearfully, as if she dreaded that the voice would be silent and break off for her this sudden, incredible renewal of all her hopes.

"It's not yet time for him to see you, Lydia, much as he wants to. But you must do something for him . . . to help both him and yourself."

"W-what is it?" she gasped.

"Do you remember the old white house back in Trubecke?" The hoarseness of that unknown voice had tautened now with an eagerness; somehow, it no longer terrified her.

"Oh, yes! So very much!"

"And the attic—your father said you used to play there when you were a child."

"I did! Yes, I remember!"

"Go back to that house, Lydia. You will meet him there. First, you must look in the attic. Before he left— before he was made to leave——" (There was a moment's pause between those two phrases which made the young brunette shiver from a feeling that a wind had suddenly blown over her own grave.) "—he wrote a long story about what was happening in Trubecke."

"But—but would it still be there, after all these years? A—Aunt Corinne moved some of the furniture here and sold a good deal—she told me she did——"

"Your father thought you would ask me that, Lydia." Once again there was a pause. "Yes, it's possible the story's gone now. Perhaps even that it was found by somebody else. But, if you find it, you'll find the truth."

Suspicion swiftly rose to Lydia's dazed mind; she groped now for reassurance and reaffirmation of what an unknown voice had told her. "Why didn't he go back and find it, then?"

"He thought you would ask that, too, Lydia." The voice was gentler now. "It's still too dangerous for him to go back to Trubecke."

"Dangerous? But why?"

"He made enemies there, Lydia. Enemies who still remember him with hate, even after eight years. Because he put them into his writing, held them up for others to see, and they won't forgive him for that, ever, even believing him dead."

Lydia's suspicions eased somewhat, for she remembered having overheard Aunt Corinne's telling her father how he was adding to his unpopularity by his uncompromising writing. She asked, "C-can't you tell me where he is now?"

"He thinks it wiser that you don't know, Lydia. In the event that anyone might try to stop you from going back to Trubecke, it's best if you are not able to tell them where to find him. And, one thing more——"

"Oh, what is it? I want to see him. I've missed him so much all these years—if you see him, will you tell him that?"

"Yes, Lydia, I'll tell him. Now, listen, this one last thing—he had a friend—Jim Lawlor, married, with two young sons. Jim was a faithful friend. And, when you go back to Trubecke, Jim will be there waiting for you—to hire you as a nurse for his little boys. They're ten and twelve, and their names are Peter and Michael."

"Peter and Michael—yes—I'll remember. But——"

"He has two grown sons, too, twenty-two and twenty-four, and their names are Ray and John Ray's doing graduate work at U.C.L.A., but John will be there. So will his mother Marge. Remember those names."

"I—I don't quite understand——"

"In time, everything will be explained to you, Lydia. Trust me. Trust your father."

"Oh, I do, I do! But—you say I'm to go back to Trubecke and work for Mr. Lawlor as a nurse for Peter and Michael? I—I haven't any money to get out there, and I don't want to borrow from Aunt Corinne——"

"No, that you mustn't do. And it would be best if you

didn't tell her where or when you're going. Again, you must take your father's word for what I'm telling you."

How strangely the stranger spoke, with an earnestness that somehow reassured her that this was not a jest.

"Y-yes, I will. When am I to go?" Lydia asked.

"As quickly as you can. The money—let me see. Go to the East Side Air Terminal tomorrow afternoon, and ask at the United Air Lines ticket counter for an envelope in your name. It will have money for your flight to Los Angeles and from there to Bakersfield, as well as enough to hire a cab to take you on to Trubecke. Is that clear?"

Now her heart was pounding like a trip-hammer with the excitement and mystery of this imminent journey, one which was to be kept a secret from even Aunt Corinne.

"Yes, I'll remember everything," she eagerly promised. "But—but where will I find this Mr. Lawlor and the boys I'm to care for?"

"They'll be staying at the Trubecke Hotel, under the name of 'Lawson.' Don't forget that name, Lydia, *not* 'Lawlor.' Because Jim Lawlor is a newspaper man as your father was, and he's famous throughout California for his editorials and feature stories. If he were known by his real name in Trubecke, public attention might be aroused about him and, in turn, about your father."

"I—I understand."

"In the envelope at the ticket counter, Lydia, you'll find a note which will have all that I've told you written down so you won't forget. But be careful. And don't tell anyone in New York that you're going. Now, I'll hang up."

"Wait, please, before——"

But the line was dead.

Greatly troubled, feeling as if she had just wakened from an impossible dream, Lydia replaced the French phone on the stand.

Chapter Eleven

LYDIA WALKED slowly back into the living room, trying to establish some composure and think what she must do. For eight years, she had been the docile, well-behaved companion and ward of her domineering aunt. And, in all that time, her only impulsive act had been to enroll in nursing school; she had even gone so far as to ask her aunt for a loan for the tuition fee. She had paid it nearly all back, too, saving what she could out of the small allowance Aunt Corinne gave her and the money she had earned for reading to Mrs. Burnan. But, in all other things, she had been the dutiful, acquiescent niece.

Now, within the span of a single day, she found herself staggered and undecided by the discovery—first of her father's book, then the poem, and now the revelation, through this mysterious phone call, that her father was still alive! More than this, the unknown caller had offered her a way to return to the town where she had known the happiest of childhoods—a place which, in her young womanhood, had until today seemed as remote and forgotten in her scheme of things as the Cape of Good Hope.

Tomorrow, an envelope with money for her fare back to Trubecke would be waiting for her. That was what the caller had said. If this were a cruel trick someone was playing on her, then there would be no envelope, no money. She considered the business about her father's friend and his two young sons waiting for her in Trubecke under an assumed name. What did that have to do with her father, or with her?

Perplexed, Lydia sat down at the writing desk. It was very dark out now. The storm had ended. Once again, the panorama of lights stretched out beyond her, sharp, clear, dazzling her—as they never failed to do—with the vastness of the city. And she thought again of the attic which looked out on dull, scorched ground in the summer, set down in that lonely kind of wilderness, with so few houses around to break the listless monotony of the scenery. The house would be dusty and empty after all these years, more of a sepulcher than the once happy abode where she had grown up as a child fortunate in knowing that her parents loved her.

How would she explain all this to Aunt Corinne? The caller had warned her not to tell anyone about her return to Trubecke, not even her aunt. Assuming that she went, what would her aunt say when she came back? To what could she attribute a sudden disappearance without explanation?

And yet . . . and yet . . . even the slimmest hope that this caller was telling the truth, was worth pursuing. In all logic, in all cold fact, she had not seen her father's corpse, not attended his funeral, not been able personally to affirm that he was really dead. There had been only her aunt's word that he was—that, and the eight years of hearing nothing. Wasn't that proof enough that he was dead? There was a law . . . wasn't it called the "Enoch Arden" law? After seven years, a man could be called legally dead if his heirs and kin heard nothing from him, did not see him, failed to trace him by every means of employing police or private detectives. And it was eight years now since Aunt Corinne had come to her and told her that her father had driven away that night in his old Plymouth and never came back because he had been killed in a suicidal crash.

The envelope with the money for her fare to Trubecke would be waiting . . . tomorrow afternoon, it would be waiting. But tomorrow was her day with Mrs.

Burnan. Mrs. Burnan had asked her to come back tomorrow and read again to her. Yes . . . but that would be in the morning, and she would be finished, at the latest, by three. She could take a subway train down to the East Side Air Terminal and ask at the United Air Lines counter for the envelope. If it wasn't there, she would know this had all been a sadistic hoax. Yet all it would have done, then, really, would have been to make her mourn her father all over again. And that was something she would not regret, not when she had at last read the book which set forth so beautifully, so touchingly, the story of his coming to that little California town and meeting her beautiful, gentle mother. She would mourn him much more deeply now, after knowing his creative gifts that had been stilled by death.

Yet—what if the caller had been telling the truth? What if Father were really alive? How he was, she hadn't the faintest idea. What if the envelope with the money was waiting for her when she went to claim it? What would she do then?

Lydia knew she would go out there, even if it meant that the caller had carried his macabre joke to the cruelest possible lengths to torture and taunt her. If there were the slightest chance of seeing her father again, with that twinkle in his blue eyes and the quick little smile he had always for her, she would go into the jungles of the Amazon.

How dark it was now. And how lonely she felt, sitting here at the window, all by herself in the apartment. But she had to think. She mustn't let Aunt Corinne know anything about the call. Because Aunt Corinne would be sure to say she was having hallucinations and then she would be certain to argue, and, the next thing, her aunt would say something particularly spiteful against her father.

There was a slim red wax candle in the silver candlestick. It hadn't been damaged at all when the candle-

85

stick had fallen to the floor. She'd light it. It would give the illusion of cheerfulness and intimacy. Sometimes her father and mother, sitting in the library and spooning—that was what they had done, and she had always thought it so heartwarming and not at all silly (as Beckie or Gloria would have termed it if she had ever told them about it)—would light a candle and sit there on the couch holding hands and watching the flicker of the tiny flame.

There must be matches in the drawer of the desk somewhere. Lydia pulled open the broad top drawer by both its brass handles. She had seen Aunt Corinne sitting here many times, smoking cigarettes. There was even a little glass ash tray opposite the candlestick, so, somewhere, there would be matches. Aunt Corinne was never one to make omissions that would lead to inconvenience and discomfort for herself.

Lydia put her slim fingers into the bottom of the drawer, tentatively groping. A little box—no, those were paperclips. Maybe at the back. There—she'd found a packet. She pulled back her hand, drew out the packet, and, as she did so, something fluttered down to the floor. Her hand had rubbed over a piece of paper and dragged it out along with the matches. She leaned down to pick it up. It was a piece of yellow paper. A telegram. And it had fallen so that the message faced her when she picked it up; she couldn't help seeing it. It was dated May Fifteenth of the current year, not quite two weeks ago, and it was from Bakersfield.

She had had no intention of reading it, for her parents had brought her up to regard other people's mail or private papers as their inviolate property. They, in turn, had scrupulously maintained the same standard for themselves; for, as a little girl, she had sent away for little novelty toys and children's books, and they had always given her the mail addressed to "Miss Lydia Turner" without ever having opened it. But, in picking the telegram up, she had automatically glanced at it . . . a short message, and still shorter, cryptic signature:

CORINNE EDWARDS
PARK SEVENTY APARTMENTS
NEW YORK CITY

PAYMENTS TOO FAR APART. BETTER FLY OUT FOR HEAR-
ING. NO TRICKS IF YOU WANT TO DIVVY WARD'S ESTATE.

LEX

Lydia read it again, hypnotically drawn by the phrase "DIVVY WARD'S ESTATE." It meant—it meant herself. For she was Aunt Corinne's ward. But who was "LEX"? And how could there be an estate when her mother's will had left money to Aunt Corinne and her father had left only enough to see her through school and preliminary nurse's training?

Unless Aunt Corinne hadn't told her the entire truth —Lydia knew very little about the law. Each state had its own laws concerning inheritance. In California, a hus- band and wife shared equally, hence, the term "com- munity property." But she had always thought that a child of deceased parents would take precedence over any other kin. Yet Aunt Corinne had made a point of telling her, not once, but several times, that her dead mother had left a will which turned over almost all of the latter's part of the estate to her, not to Lydia.

But, if this telegram meant what her first swift glance had assimilated, then Aunt Corinne had lied. For the telegram spoke of a ward's estate to be divided, in the present tense, which was now. She was the ward—there was none other over whom her aunt had jurisdiction. And if that were true, then the estate had not been "used up" in putting her through high school and in giving her that year of training at the Hospital of the Angels—a year for which she had borrowed two hundred and fifty

87

dollars from her aunt. She had repaid the tuition loan, proudly believing that she was demonstrating a measure of independence by saving what money she earned in her occasional jobs as a practical nurse and giving it back to Aunt Corinne, who lived without stint or economy.

Was it possible that Aunt Corinne had been living on money that was rightfully hers?

As she shoved the telegram back into the drawer, trying to reposition it as she had unwittingly come upon it, Lydia made a decision. She would follow the instructions of the unknown caller. And, if there really were an envelope at the United Air Lines counter, as he had promised, she would go back to Trubecke. If Aunt Corinne had deceived her all these years, then she had been right in her instinctive rebellion today against her aunt's disparaging judgment against her father. Even if the trail back to Trubecke should prove to be no more than a dead end, she would try to begin over again by herself and live her own life. She had been a servant much too long to a parasitical, selfish woman. If she had to be a servant, henceforth, it would be to the sick and the needy. Even if she had to do menial labor to earn money to finish her schooling, she would become a registered nurse and try to make up for these wasted years.

Chapter Twelve

Lydia could hardly sleep that night. Long after her aunt had come in, a little after midnight, she lay in bed reviewing the curiously entangled skein of incidents. She had pretended to be asleep when Aunt Corinne entered the apartment, if only to avoid the inevitable grumbling complaints at such a late hour. She knew them in advance: lateness for dinner, having to hurry with each course and not to be able to enjoy it leisurely, having to call a cab by herself, the draftiness of the theater, the poor angle of the seat she had been assigned, the imperfect acoustics, the storm—a parade of inconsequential minutiae which, in her aunt's lexicon, added up to a disastrous evening.

She had heard Aunt Corinne walk softly to the door of her room and call out in a stage whisper: "Are you asleep, dear?" And then, after a moment, she'd walked away. Lydia had restlessly turned over and told herself she simply must go to sleep if she expected to read for Mrs. Burnan and then get back into the heart of town without Aunt Corinne's guessing what errand would keep her so long.

She wouldn't pack, of course. She'd wear her best dress and her cloth coat, the light one, because it would already be in the nineties out in Trubecke. No—not the dress. If she were going back to the town where she was born and where she didn't want to be recognized—although she knew that she did not resemble the rather tall, thin, serious child of twelve which she had been at the time of her departure—it would be better to wear the nurse's uniform and cap. After all, if she were going to work as a nurse or governess for Mr. Lawlor's—Lawson's—two small boys, the uniform would be more in keeping with the role she was being asked to play.

A role to play. It would be almost like an allegory—a kind of allegory such as her father's novel had portrayed. What would be its ending? And who was "LEX" and how did he fit into the story? It was while she was pondering this baffling new element that fatigue claimed her and at last her eyes closed and the boon of sleep was finally granted her . . .

"Oh, how nice!" Her aunt sat up in bed, frowningly passing a hand over her forehead. Her eyes were puffy and the corners of her mouth turned down—sure signs that last night had not been without flaw.

"I've made the coffee strong and black, the way you like it, Aunt Corinne." Lydia gently placed the little tray on her aunt's lap. She had wakened at seven-thirty, made her own breakfast, looked in on her aunt, and observed that the latter was beginning to stir and to moan —again, infallible signs that she would soon be awake— and gone back to the kitchen to prepare coffee, dark rye bread toast with blackberry jam and a peeled orange— Aunt Corinne's favorite breakfast after a lucullan repast the night before.

"You're so very thoughtful, dear." Aunt Corinne, disregarding the little paring knife on the plate beside the orange, took it in both hands and broke it expertly in half. Then she crammed one of the halves into her mouth and chewed, sighing with hedonistic enjoyment at the cool tartness. Lydia looked away so as not to be a witness to this display of gluttony . . . and also so that she could control her own feelings; she had so long affected a meek docility before Aunt Corinne that any show of excitement or secret feverish vitality would have been suspicious.

So, continuing to act her role—for this time she was

conscious of acting it, now that she had determined that, come what may, she would soon be free of this existence —Lydia placatingly murmured, after an interval sufficient to allow her aunt to masticate and swallow, "I do hope your dinner and the show weren't spoiled, Aunt Corinne."

"Umph, don't talk about it!" Her aunt reached for the coffee cup and took a noisy sip, slushing it about in her mouth, then swallowing. Lydia tried not to wince.

"Of course, you know, it was all your fault. If you'd not gone into tantrums and had awakened me when you ought to have, I shouldn't have had to rush through the meal. As it was, they were out of the kidneys, so I ordered *Scaloppine con Marsala e Funghi*. Of course, I made them rush it—but it wasn't cooked enough to my taste, so I had to send it back—I was nearly out of my mind—and then, after that awful storm, cabs were scarce as hens' teeth—I finally got one, and I was five minutes late. Then I had the wretched luck to sit next to two of the gabbiest women I ever met, and they talked all through the first act—oh, my dear, it was ghastly!" She threw up her hands and shook her head, while Lydia clucked her tongue and murmured a suitably sympathetic phrase. "Now, this afternoon, dear, I want you to go shopping with me. I need some shoes, some really elegant pumps for the theater. And I'd love to bring home half a dozen of those huge brioches from Colette's Bakery, and there's a darling hat I saw in the Bloomingdale ad——"

"I—I'm afraid I can't. Not today, Aunt Corinne."

"Oh?" A peevish voice, the corners of the small ripe mouth turning down more than ever. "And why not? You don't have any work today. You go to Mrs. Burnan's again tomorrow, as usual, don't you?"

Lydia shook her head. "Usually, yes, Aunt Corinne. But, yesterday, she especially said she wanted me to come back again today."

"Oh, she did. Well, I dare say you'll have to go. But you won't be all day. You never are, you know. You might at least take pity on me, after the trouble you caused me last night, and meet me downtown the minute you finish with that silly old woman."

It was on the tip of Lydia's tongue to say that Mrs. Burnan deserved the least, of all the adjectives possible to characterize her, the one Aunt Corinne had so deprecatingly chosen and that, indeed, it would be better applied to Aunt Corinne herself. But she could tell from the petulance of her aunt's mouth and the self-pitying tiny sighs that had accompanied that last speech that any such candor would mean disaster. So she meekly replied, as if she were accepting the tirade as a personal rebuke, "I'll try, Aunt Corinne. I usually finish about three or a little before. Where should I meet you?"

"Hmph! By then, the afternoon's nearly gone, as you well know, and cabs are hard to find. You make it so *difficult* for me sometimes, Lydia, I really don't know what's got into you lately," her aunt complained. Then she munched a piece of toast and washed it down with the rest of the coffee before she deigned to formulate her plans. "Oh, very well. I suppose you can't disappoint her —and she *is* steady pay. I know you want to earn your own money, which is very commendable. Let me think —I'll get my shoes at I. Miller's, then lunch at La Fonda del Sol—I simply must try their wonderful Mexican chocolate candy cake—then to the bakery—well, suppose you meet me at Bloomingdale's, on the first floor, by the perfume section? But don't be any later than three —try to get away. I should think that old woman would be bored after she's heard you read a couple of hours. I know I would be."

"Yes, Aunt Corinne." Lydia, eyes dutifully lowered, ignored the obvious slur.

"All right. Now you can draw the water for a bath for me. I'd like it just a bit more than mild, but not too hot, mind you. And get out my blue floral silk dress, that's a lamb. Oh, before you do, might I have just another bite of toast and jam, and more coffee?"

Mrs. Burnan was in a nostalgic mood that morning. She had just had an airmail letter from Charles. He had employed all his considerable, if shallow, charm to write her a lyrically effusive letter about the charms of Paris in the spring, with more than one delicately direct suggestion that these charms would be more enjoyable if one had a thick sheaf of the new hundred-franc notes to expend on them. He had submitted two oils to a dealer near Montmartre, who thought highly of them. He was going through the same "blue period" that Picasso had experienced, and, at last, he felt his creative soul was initiating an heroic struggle for liberation.

Della Hargell had already brought the checkbook and pen and was steadying her mistress's hand so that Charles' plea would not go unheeded when Lydia arrived. Della ushered her in and then went back to helping Letitia Burnan make out the check.

"Good morning, Lydia, dear," Letitia Burnan turned her smiling face towards the young brunette. "Isn't it a beautiful day? I can feel it in the air from the window, and the warm sun. After a storm, it usually turns out well, doesn't it?"

"Yes, Mrs. Burnan. I—I want to thank you for giving me that book yesterday. I—I read it as soon as I got back home. It—it was a lovely story, and it's so much like the way I remember my parents."

"I'm so glad, my dear. All right, Della, put that in an envelope and send it off airmail."

"Regular mail would make him wait and appreciate it more, Mrs. Burnan," Della grumbled.

Letitia Burnan smiled and shrugged. "You know perfectly well he'd be cabling if you didn't send it airmail. Poor Charles is much too impulsive."

"You talk about him as if he were still a child of ten, Mrs. Burnan." Della sniffed. "And he's closer to fifty than I am."

"Tush, tush," her employer softly chided. "As long as I can think of him as a small well-meaning boy, I don't think about my own age, which is just as well. Now, Lydia, I'd like to hear some more poetry again today, if you don't mind. From the same volume."

"I'll get it right away, Mrs. Burnan." Lydia brought the volume back and seated herself in the chair Della had already placed near the wheelchair. "There we are, now. What poems would you like today?"

"Why don't you choose them for me, Lydia, dear? You read so beautifully, with such meaning. Ah, you'd have made a wonderful schoolteacher. I know. I used to be one myself—oh, not with your patience, though, dear. I was on my way to being a tyrant, I think—I was so eager to drum some zest for living and learning into my pupils' heads. But you wouldn't be like that. You'd be gentle and helpful—that's your nature."

"You're right, there, for once," Della unexpectedly chimed in, with a brisk nod at Lydia, who flushed at the rare compliment.

"Maybe I ought to have kept on being a tyrant, with Charles anyway." Mrs. Burnan sighed, leaning her head back as if recalling the past. "Ah, well, to use one of the proverbs from the country in which Charles finds himself these days—if youth but knew, if age but could. All right, that's enough philosophizing. Now, let's hear from the master of poets, Lydia dear."

Della coughed behind her hand. "I'll be outside if you need me, Mrs. Burnan." She left the library, closing the door behind her.

Meanwhile, Lydia had opened the thick volume at random while Mrs. Burnan had been reminiscing. Looking down at the page she had marked, she saw the heading,

"The Poor Relation." And as Della left the room, she glanced at the stanzas. And these lines stood out:

> Beneath her beauty, blanched with pain,
> And wistful yet for being cheated,
> A child would seem to ask again
> A question many times repeated;
> But no rebellion has betrayed
> Her wonder at what she has paid
> For memories that have no stain,
> For triumph born to be defeated.*

"Have you found something yet, dear?" Mrs. Burnan turned towards the young brunette.

"Wistful yet for being cheated"—is it true? Have I been cheated? Did Aunt Corinne keep the money that was rightfully mine and lie to me about it? "But no rebellion has betrayed"—no, because I've been meek and mild and done everything Aunt Corinne wanted. But not any more. I'm going back to Trubecke today. Yes, today. And I'm going to find out what happened to my father. And if it turns out that it's a lie and he's really dead, I'll find out all I can for myself, so I'll know.

"N-no, Mrs. Burnan, not yet. There are so many lovely poems, I can't make up my mind. Wait a minute——" Lydia turned the pages again, and then stopped, her eyes widening. Was it a sign? Because she had turned to page 81, and the poem which appeared there was "The House on the Hill." It began:

> They are all gone away,
>   The House is shut and still,
> There is nothing more to say.

---

* "The Poor Relation," reprinted with permission of The Macmillan Company, copyright 1916 by E. A. Robinson, renewed 1944 by Ruth Nivison.

Through broken walls and gray
    The winds blow bleak and shrill:
They are all gone away.

Nor is there one to-day
    To speak them good or ill:
There is nothing more to say.*

A chill of premonition seized Lydia. Was this paragraph prophetic? Was she destined to go back to a deserted house for an answer that did not exist?

Seeing Mrs. Burnan's face tauten with expectancy and concern, she turned the pages again, frantically searching for a verse that would have no link to the chain of her anxious, jangled thoughts.

"Oh, here we are—how about 'Isaac and Archibald,' Mrs. Burnan?"

"Oh, yes." The drawn solicitous lines of the craggy old face relaxed. "That's a charming poem, my dear. Do begin with that. It takes me back to when I was a child myself."

And Lydia began to read about the two old men who, each in turn, took a small boy aside and confided to their young companion that each was afraid that the other was failing fast. But, even in this bucolic, tenderly wistful poem there was a nuance with uncanny immediacy for the young brunette's distraught ruminations.

For the child in the poem, the child made confidante by those two kindly old men, was twelve years old, as she had been when her mother had died so tragically.

* "The House on the Hill," from *The Children of the Night,* by Edwin Arlington Robinson, Charles Scribner's Sons, New York, 1890.

Chapter Thirteen

THE READING session might well have extended into late afternoon, so absorbed was Letitia Burnan in Lydia's rendition of poetry, if the brunette had not pleaded a prior appointment to meet her aunt in Manhattan. As it was, it was not till a few minutes before three that Lydia was able to leave the brownstone house, and, at twenty minutes of four, she entered the East Side Terminal and went up to the United Air Lines ticket counter.

A vivacious redhead in the trim blue cap and uniform of the airline smiled at the lovely brunette. Lydia had worn her white nurse's uniform and cap and was carrying her light cloth coat.

"May I help you?" the redhead inquired.

"Do—do you have an envelope here for Lydia Turner?"

"Let me check for you." The redhead pulled open a drawer and expertly ran a slim finger over the alphabetically listed ticket envelopes. Not finding it there, she looked in the back of the drawer. "Why, yes, here you are."

"T-thank you." Lydia took the brown business envelope and walked over to a nearby bench to examine its contents.

Then it wasn't a hoax. But wait—maybe there was nothing in the envelope.

She tore it open with trembling fingers. No, it was no hoax. Inside within a folded sheet of paper, were three crisp new one-hundred dollar bills. And on the sheet was typed a message . . . a message which verified all

97

that the caller had told her last night on the telephone: Jim Lawlor's assumed name at the hotel in Trubecke, the appointed rendezvous with her father, the admonition to search in the attic for evidence which would explain her father's actions during his last few terrible months. And repeated instructions on the swiftest course back to Trubecke.

Lydia's last doubt vanished. She would go back to the old white house. No matter what she learned there, she would free herself once and for all from the bondage of servitude which Aunt Corinne had so unfeelingly imposed upon her. She rose and went back to the ticket counter, where the redhead was just hanging up the phone.

"Can—can I get space on a plane to Los Angeles and transfer to Bakersfield?" Lydia asked. Glancing at her wrist watch, she inwardly winced to think of how Aunt Corinne must be fuming by now. It was almost an hour past the time that she had promised to meet her aunt at Bloomingdale's.

"You've just missed a jet flight, Miss Turner——"

Lydia stiffened, wide-eyed and wary. She stammered, "How—how did you know my name?"

"That's easy." The redhead laughed, showing perfect white teeth. "You just asked for an envelope for Lydia Turner, and you opened it and read it. So I naturally assumed you're she. Am I right?"

"Oh, y—yes—you are." Lydia blushed. *How thoughtless she'd been not to remember that—but the caller had told her on the phone that she was not to tell anyone in New York of her departure.*

"Good! It's our pleasure to give you personalized service. That's why I wanted to be sure of your name, Miss Turner. Now let's see. The next nonstop jet to L.A. would be Flight Number Fifteen, which leaves at 6:30 P.M. from Kennedy, arriving at L.A. at 9 P.M. Then you'd connect with a Convair, Flight 582, leaving L.A.

at 10:25 P.M., arriving at Bakersfield at 11:11 P.M. Your jet is a DC-8, and it's a dinner flight, of course."

"I—I think I'd like to take that —is that the quickest service there is out there, Miss?"

"I'm afraid it is, Miss Turner. Shall I book you on those flights?"

"Y-yes. How much is it? Oh, one thing more—do you know if there are cabs in Bakersfield that would take me to—to—a small town about thirty miles from there?"

"I, personally, don't, Miss Turner. But I can wire our Bakersfield office and find out for you. To make the 6:30 flight this evening out ought to be here at the Terminal no later than 5:45, and I certainly ought to have a reply for you by then."

"Y-you're very kind. Thank you."

The redhead smiled at the lovely young nurse. "It's my job, and I like people, Miss Turner. But you mustn't give me too much personal credit. United has the largest aviation communications center in the world to obtain information for paying passengers. I'll teletype your request in at once. Now, let me write the ticket up for you —you asked about cost—that'll be $168.95 including tax for the flight from Kennedy to Los Angeles, and then $10.29 including tax from L.A. to Bakersfield . . . a total of $179.24, Miss Turner. Out of two hundred. And thank you for choosing United. By the time you're ready to board our limousine for Kennedy, I'll have that information you wanted about cabs. Here are your tickets and your change, and have a very pleasant trip."

"T-thank you so very much," Lydia said gratefully.

As she turned away, she bumped into a tall man carrying a brief case and wearing an expensively tailored gray nylon suit and jaunty homburg.

"Oh, I beg your pardon, sir—I'm sorry——"

"Quite all right, Miss. Hope I didn't jostle you too hard?"

His hair was closely cropped and steely gray. His blue eyes were pleasantly quizzical. He had almost no brows, and where the left brow would have been, there was a jagged dark-purplish scar. Another scar, wider and paler, marked the undercurve of his chin. His mouth was ascetically thin, and, when he smiled as he asked the question, Lydia observed that he had a complete set of false teeth—they must have been, she reasoned, since they were all perfectly aligned and without fillings. And he wore thick-lensed spectacles.

"Oh, no, you didn't."

Lydia gave him a polite smile and nod and walked back to the bench. *It would be wiser to stay here till the limousine was ready to leave, have a snack at the restaurant, and not risk being seen out on the street. She was sure Aunt Corinne wouldn't guess where she'd gone after leaving Mrs. Burnan's; she'd been very careful not to say a word about her plans. Wait a minute—when Mrs. Burnan had asked her to come back Friday, she'd said she wasn't sure she could and she'd phone Della the evening before. Well, even if Aunt Corinne called at the Burnan house, and found out what she'd told Mrs. Burnan, she wouldn't be able to figure out what Lydia had meant.*

The man in the gray nylon suit and homburg walked up to the United ticket counter where the redhead presided, tipped his hat and began to talk to her. In a few minutes, she began to write out a ticket for him. As he took out his Morocco leather wallet to pay her, he looked back at the bench on which Lydia sat, rapt in thought, holding her cloth coat on her lap.

He studied her, his eyes squinting through the thick lenses of the hornrimmed spectacles, his face impassive. Then he turned back to the redhead.

Chapter Fourteen

Now THAT she was resolved, with no more vacillation or submissiveness, to set forth on this flight back into the past, back into the darkness of memory so that its mysteries and speculations could no longer conceal themselves, Lydia felt a mounting tension and impatience at having to wait even the two and a half hours till the big DC-8 jet would soar westward. And, too, the reaction of sober reflection had begun to set in after this secretive, swiftly rash decision. When she had torn open that brown envelope and found the money and the note, she had had reassurance to alleviate her wavering doubts, dispersion of her suspicions that the plan had all been a malicious joke.

With the ticket envelope, the hundred dollar bill and the change from the other two bills in her purse, the overt act of breaking with the life she had led with Aunt Corinne was at an end. But its consequences might not be. She bought a magazine at the newsstand and read it, though without concentration, simply to pass the time away. And she looked up constantly at the big electric clock on the wall to urge the hour and the minute hands, through the sheer yearning of her will, to move more swiftly. She looked up, too, whenever she heard people walking towards her. Her fingers trembled as they turned the pages of the magazine. At any moment, she expected an enraged Aunt Corinne to storm into the Air Terminal looking for her.

The big purse with its sturdy carrying strap might have been a temptation to a thief following her along a crowded street, but Lydia found it now an ally as well as a convenience. When she had left the Park Avenue apartment this morning to go to Mrs. Burnan's, she had slipped the prayer book and the copy of her father's novel into its roomy depths, safely out of view. The novel would not have fitted into either pocket of the cloth coat. And if she had carried it under her arm, Aunt Corinne might have asked why she was taking it along to her job, when she had already read it. Pent up with excitement and tension as she had been, after a restless night, Lydia doubted that her powers of conspiracy would have enabled her to remain calm in the face of her aunt's nagging inquisitions—she had endured too many of them in the past. Even when she could face them calmly, with no such emotional burden as possessed her at this moment, she had often been sorely taxed to maintain the placid docility which was her custom.

The minutes dragged with agonizing slowness. The murmur of conversation, the sound of people quickening their steps towards the exit where the limousines waited to take them to the airports, the clatter of baggage being set down on weighing scales, the ringing of phones, cumulatively augmented into a deafening clamor in Lydia's ears. The magazine, forgotten, dropped to the floor at her feet; her eyes, haunted, fearful, sought the entrances and exits, sought the inexorably—but, oh, so slowly—moving clock.

At last it was time to leave for Flight Number Fifteen; over the public address system, a courteous, calm voice, speaking with succinctness in a tone that Lydia envied for its composure and reassurance, announced the readiness of the limousine servicing that cross-country flight. She rose, wavering from enervation; the muscles of her calves writhed and threatened for a moment to give way; then, at last, she found herself walking forward with the other passengers, the strap of her purse over her shoulder like a veteran traveler, carrying her cloth coat.

She glanced at herself as she walked in line to enter the limousine. It was incongruous, this uniform of hers; the white badge of care for the sick, the aged, the young in pain. Cap, uniform, white stockings, and white shoes, as if she were being flown across country to a sickbed where a gravely ill patient awaited her. But this was not the case; this was by way of masquerade. Yet it was not a masquerade of farce or wit, but one which, paradoxically, would in turn unmask another, perhaps deadly serious, masquerade. For, if her father were actually still alive, and if her aunt had actually cheated her of her inheritance, then, somehow, there had been a crime committed. If not murder—it could not have been murder if her father lived—some hidden kind of evil conspiracy to let her grow to maturity believing that she was penniless and orphaned and must depend on the contemptuous charity of Aunt Corinne.

Just before she stepped into the limousine, one hand touching her purse to make sure it was still intact, she quickly glanced back over her shoulder. Her dark brown eyes were wide and fear-shadowed, her lips parted, as if any instant she expected to see her aunt, with a policeman in tow, coming after her. Yet, at the same time, she recognized this as a childish irrational fear. Logical, unperturbed thinking told her—as she had insisted to herself all during that seemingly endless wait on the bench at the Air Terminal—that there was no way conceivable that her aunt could have guessed where she was going; no, not even if she had called Mrs. Burnan's house and learned from Della that her niece had said she wasn't sure she could come Friday. Every measured fact gleaned from sober reflection stood in Lydia's favor—but she still could not rid herself of a nagging dread. A dread of what? If her father was alive, it was a time for joy and tears of happiness and thanks unto God that he had been spared to her, a time for planning how to make up those lost years during which each had been denied the

103

other's love and understanding. And yet . . . and yet. . . .

There was no sign of Aunt Corinne. But, in that glance, hasty, haunted, and surely illogically compelled, she had time to see that the man standing behind her was the one in the gray nylon suit and homburg with the brief case, the man whom she had bumped into after buying her ticket. He gave her no sign of recognition other than the most imperceptible of nods, his thin lips hardly moving in the faintest ghost of a smile.

Then, taking a deep breath, Lydia clambered into the limousine, chose a seat at the back, and closed her eyes, as if willing herself to shut out any thoughts of negation; till the moment she actually boarded the DC-8, till the moment it hurtled into the air towards the west and the rendezvous with the old white house. She still could not quite believe all this was happening.

The limousine pulled out of the terminal. Briefly she opened her eyes, to ascertain the movement, then again closed them. That brief glimpse had shown her the two rows of seats, half filled with passengers, all with their backs to her, and no one boarding to come for her.

Then the lights of the great airport, the sight of planes taxiing out on the runway, and the natural, surging excitement as the reality of this impulsive, unchartered, unreasoned adventure grew within her, momentarily driving away the last clinging wisps of uncertainty and uneasiness. It would be a new experience. She had never flown in a jet plane; it would more than halve the time consumed in a propeller plane . . . in five and a half short hours, she would be in California; three more, and she would be back in the little town where she had been born. The friendly, helpful redheaded ticket agent had told her, just before she boarded the limousine, that it would be possible to hire a cab in Bakersfield to take her to her destination. And Lydia, who had never before resorted to ruses or deceit, felt a tiny glow of triumph at having been adroit enough to keep from mentioning the actual name of the town—

But wait—she told the girl she was going to a town about thirty miles from Bakersfield. If anyone were to inquire at the United ticket counter, anyone who knew her, like Aunt Corinne, and learn that a girl in a nurse's uniform and cap had asked about cabs from Bakersfield to a town that many miles away, it would be all too easy to deduce that it had been Trubecke she had meant. She bit her lips with vexation. In her new freedom, brief though it might be, she was like a child after all. What were those last lines of "The Poor Relation"?

> Unsought, unthought-of, and unheard,
> She sings and watches like a bird,
> Safe in a comfortable cage
> From which there will be no more flying.*

Yes. Ingenuous as she was, if this poor stratagem were to fail, she would be returned to that safety, her freedom again curtailed.

No—no matter what the outcome of this clandestine flight, she would begin again, even if she had to scrub dishes in a cheap hamburger stand; she would save every penny and continue her training as a nurse, so that ultimately she could be of use, of service, to the needy. Only thus could she make up for this vegetational existence. Her father's novel had dwelt on the theme that it is man's duty to search for truth and honor, and that love—not just the physical, but the timeless welding of compatible psyches—is at the end of that consecrated quest. It was an unworldly theme by modern, cynical standards, but Lydia clung to it. Even as a young aspirant nurse, she

* E. A. Robinson, "The Poor Relation," *The Man Against the Sky*, The Macmillan Company, New York, 1916.

had seen enough of cruelty and suffering, yet she felt that on the eternal balance scales the good would out-weigh the evil.

Otherwise, life was meaningless. If the world was to fawn over the ruthless and the parasites of great wealth and scoff at the dreamers and the idealists, and if the former were to triumph, all the teachings of the wise and sober through the centuries were dross. And that she could not, would not, accept. Take Robinson, the poet whom Mrs. Burnan loved so deeply and for whose writings her own father had had such an affinity. By material standards, he was a comparative failure. Yet, while she had read to the blind woman in the brownstone house, often her eyes had filled with tears at the exquisite perception of his vision.

The lines of "The Man Against the Sky," which she had read that afternoon to Mrs. Burnan, came back to her now . . .

> Where was he going, this man against the sky?
> You know not, nor do I.
> But this we know, if we know anything:
> That we may laugh and fight and sing
> And of our transience here make offering
> To an orient Word that will not be erased,
> Or, save in incommunicable gleams
> Too permanent for dreams,
> Be found or known.*

Lydia drew a deep breath, straightening her shoulders, and boarded the jet. And, this time, she didn't glance out the window, much as she was tempted, to see if anyone were coming after her.

* E. A. Robinson, *The Man Against the Sky*, The Macmillan Company, New York, 1916.

Chapter Fifteen

THE THRILLING new experience of her fist jet flight served to occupy Lydia's mind and divert her from dwelling on the past. There was nothing in her past knowledge to prepare her for the wonder and the fantasy of being borne aloft, almost without knowing it, to high cruising altitude. No vibration, no roaring of engines, no awareness even of the incredible rate of speed by which the gleaming plane slashed across distance to bring her ever nearer to her birthplace.

The excellent dinner—she declined cocktails—fortified her spiritually, too. Having been so long the self-effacing attendant at the gourmet feasts of Aunt Corinne, one whose judgment or preference was never consulted, used as a sounding board for an interminable egotistic monologue, Lydia greatly enjoyed the unaccustomed treat of dining alone, being consulted by the friendly stewardess as to her choice of coffee or tea, and asked her opinion of the highly palatable meal. Then, relaxed, she napped—and was wakened by the announcement that they were nearing Los Angeles International Airport and that all seatbelts were to be fastened.

There was an hour and a quarter ahead of her before she could board the plane to Bakersfield. To while away the time, Lydia walked about the huge building, window-shopping and observing people. There were many families with little children, either leaving the airport or coming to it. The air was warm and humid, and she overheard a cab driver, exuberantly dumping the heavy suitcases of a paunchy, well-dressed businessman into the trunk of the cab, comment with profane disgust on the smog that day.

This time her plane was a standard propeller type, far smaller than the jet, and more than half empty. She was first to board and took a seat up front. There was little to see at that hour, and the flight would take hardly more than three-quarters of an hour. Adjusting her coat on her lap, after having declined the stewardess's offer to hang it for her, Lydia made sure that the contents of her purse were intact. Yes, the novel and the prayer book were still there. She'd been so enthralled with the new experience of the jet that she hadn't once thought of reading. And now it would be pointless to start.

As she put her purse on the empty seat next to her, she looked up just in time to see the man in the gray nylon suit coming down the aisle and going past her. For just a tiny instant, a cold hand seemed to have grasped her heart and squeezed it. Recognizing him as the man whom she had noticed at the Air Terminal in New York, she thought it odd indeed that he should join her on this connection on to Bakersfield, where traffic would be relatively slight. If he had terminated his journey here in Los Angeles, there would have been no actual reason for her to be suspicious; but the coincidence of meeting, his taking the same plane to the West Coast and, now, this final one in the next to last journeying stage on to Trubecke, disconcerted her.

Again, it was time to fasten her seatbelt and to think only that by midnight she would be back home. Home, if it could still be called that, with the deserted old white house standing with its back to the moundlike hills from which Augustus Edwards had drawn enough copper to make himself rich in his lifetime and to build that then resplendent, out-of-place dwelling, one more suited to the bustling swagger of Los Angeles or the stately culture of San Francisco than arid, desolate Trubecke.

The plane set down on the Bakersfield airstrip, and she disembarked. By now Lydia was feeling tired, and she momentarily toyed with the notion of going to a hotel in town and continuing on to Trubecke in the morning. Perhaps the Lawsons—she had repeated that name to herself several times on the big jet, to be able to pronounce it without stumbling when she asked for them at the hotel in Trubecke—would have already gone to bed. Yet, so close to the house where she had been born, tired as she was, she felt a compulsion to take the final step of this transcontinental journey.

She slung the purse strap over her shoulder and walked out of the small compact air terminal building towards the row of waiting cabs. There were, in all, just three. The driver of the last one was dozing in his seat, slumped down with the bill of his cap pulled over his eyes. Lydia walked determinedly to the first in line and the driver, a short black-haired man with sunglasses and swarthy complexion, snapped to attention, got out of the cab, and opened the door to her, touching his cap and giving her a wan grin.

"Where to, lady? The El Tejon Hotel, mebbe, huh?"

Lydia glanced round. Then her eyes widened. The man with the homburg and the brief case was approaching her, going up to the cab just behind hers, and, without waiting for the driver to get out, he, himself, opened the door and got in. Lydia waited, not wanting to give her destination aloud, lest this stranger hear.

Her cabbie fidgited. "Aw, c'mon lady, have a heart, it's late 'n I been waitin' for a fare. Where you wanna go, huh? You ever been here before?"

She got inside the cab, glancing back. The man in the gray nylon suit was leaning towards his driver, saying something, and she saw the man nod. Then she realized that his cab couldn't pull out till hers did. Meanwhile, her driver, glowering now, got back behind the wheel and belligerently turned to confront her.

"Okay, now what's the mystery, huh, lady? C'mon, yer holdin' up the line!"

"Can—can you take me to Trubecke?"

"Huh? Aw, come on, lady, it's late 'n I wanna make a buck."

"I've got money. I'll pay you. But I have to go to Trubecke. Please?

"Jeez, this time a night, that's a long haul—you know whatcher askin'? Twenny-nine—meebe thirty miles —then I gotta deadhead all the way back. 'N the road's no picnic neither, not this time a night."

"I—I've got friends there—they're expecting me. Please. I said I've got money. I—I'll pay you for your time."

"Well, okay." The driver behind them angrily honked his horn. "Look—trip like that, cost ya thirty bucks. Then you gotta figger my time gittin' back with no fare, same distance, see?"

"All right—please. I—I'll give you fifty dollars. Will that be enough?" Lydia glanced back frantically at the cab behind her; the driver was now leaning on the horn and making vehement gestures with his other fist.

"Lady, you gotta deal." Her driver chuckled, and started up. Describing a broad circle, he headed the cab due northwest. Lydia looked back, her widened frightened eyes following the movements of the cab behind. She saw it start, turn at right angles, and then disappear with a sigh of relief as she settled back. The gesture with which she tossed her coat onto the seat beside her spoke of the easing of that sudden, apprehensive tension which finding the stranger of the East Side Terminal here in Bakersfield had aroused.

Chapter Sixteen

THE PROSPECT of so profitable a fare made the short, swarthy cab driver jovial, even garrulous. And, like so many of his brethren for hire behind the wheel, he was lonesome and curious. For a time, he discoursed on the hard life of a cab driver in an area of this kind, working late night shifts and rarely having the chance to talk to people. Next, he was curious about Lydia's reasons for driving to Trubecke.

"There's a real dead town. Wonder to me they don't fold up and move somewheres else," was his pithy comment.

"Why is that?" Lydia was mildly piqued. Trubecke had never been a potent factor in the rapidly expanding economic growth of California, but, from what she recalled of it—the paper box factory, the bank, the many ads in the *Reporter*—she was surprised to hear so harsh an estimate.

"For one thing, lady, there ain't much business doin' there. Nor work for people. When that factory they had there folded up coupla years back, the town sorta went to pot. Oh, they been tryin' to bring other companies down there, some minin', I hear tell, but no soap so far. I been through it once. Take it from me, it's dead. A lousy movie gets all the stinkeroos coupla years after people give up seein' them in L.A. or Frisco, coupla crummy taverns—no dames, that's for sure—some farmin'—that's the story. Now here in Bakersfield, we got oil, see, 'n it's still producin'. You got work'n you got money, you gotta real live town." He favored her

111

with a salacious wink. "So, you got friends there, huh? Now, jist where you wanna go in Trubecke?"

"To—to the hotel."

"Yeah, I know where it is. Can't miss it. Just about one main street and that's all in the whole darn town. Not too bad, only it's got run down, seein' there ain't no tourists and lotta people outa work, 'counta the factory folded, see? Your friends stayin' there, are they?"

"Y-yes."

"Un huh. You from round these parts or back East somewhere?"

"F-from New York."

Glancing out the window, Lydia shivered at the contrast before her to the teeming Manhattan streets she had quitted—how long ago had it been—about eight hours ago. Low hills and flat drab land, with only isolated small farms to break the pattern of sameness. For there was still no railroad line to connect Bakersfield with Trubecke, and a generation from now, she was certain, the same desolate, sparsely populated expanse would present itself to the wayfarer. It was a depressing thought so she quickly abandoned it.

"Now there's a live town, what I mean! Jeez, what I wouldn't give ta drive a hack in New York, lady!" The driver turned back from the wheel, an affable smile crinkling his swarthy face. All earlier resentment of her unconventional method of engaging him had been forgotten; the mention of New York had made him almost visibly deferential.

"There are a lot of them there." Lydia smiled.

"I'll bet there are, 'n I bet they need 'em bad. So you come all the way from New York, huh? Boy, them jets are the nuts, aren't they?"

For all that she was trying to put her mind into order, she couldn't be curt with the man. He was trying his best to be friendly, and it was evident that her cross-country journey had elevated her, in his eyes, into a unique

112

elite status. As a matter of fact, just as she had enjoyed the attentive meal service of the airline stewardess, so Lydia found this new attention rather flattering. At the same time, she was reminded of Aunt Corinne. Aunt Corinne would have discouraged any such conversational equality with a single withering phrase. Lydia had often heard her comment, "One has to keep menials in their place, you know, or they'd be unbearable. The first thing you know, they'd want to fraternize, and then where would you be?" She thought to herself that very possibly, even if unconsciously, her aunt had meant that kernel of wisdom for her own ears.

"Yes, they are. I left New York six-thirty their time and here I am," Lydia found herself saying, in a kind of open, if delayed, defiance of Aunt Corinne's snobbery.

"Lessee now—that's three hours ahead'a our time, ain't it—you oughta hit Trubecke around midnight, way I figger. Means you came alla way from New York in around eight hours, ain't that right? Boy, that's fast." He chuckled, shook his head. "Trubecke's gonna be sorta like a rest cure after New York, if you know what I mean. Hell—'scuse it, lady—they ain't had no excitement in that town since that big murder trial eight-nine years ago. I just came to Bakersfield outa Stockton that year, I sorta remember. Course, wouldn't mean nuttin' to you."

"M-murder trial?"

"Yeah, sure." He energetically bobbed his head, swung the wheel with a practiced hand to give a produce truck coming towards them ample leeway. "Sorta hazy right now what it was all about—you comin' all the way from the East sorta puts my mind back rememberin'. Yeah, sure, oh, some rich gal got herself knocked off, 'n they said the hubby did it, so they hadda trial in Bakersfield—sure ran a lotta stuff in the paper here about it—but they couldn't prove nuttin', so they let him go. What was the name, anyhow? I wuz drivin' a hack then too, but only

113

part time, figgerin' to get a job on a farm, but it didn't pan out—took over for the guy that had the reg'lar run, see? He came from a little dump called Webster, ain't too far from Trubecke. He wuz tellin' me this dame they think her hubby bumped off came from the family that jist about owned that jerkwater town'a Trubecke, see? Hey—I got it. Her name was 'Edwards,' only 'course she changed it when she got married."

"Wh-what about the husband?" Lydia tried hard to keep her voice from trembling.

"I dunno. Guess maybe he left town after they let him go at the trial. Never heard nuttin' after that. Least, not that I remember. But, like I wuz sayin', lady, that's about the only excitin' thing happened in Trubecke since I been drivin' a hack. Well, it won't be much longer now. Maybe 'bout five-six miles more, we'll be there. Your friends live there permanent, huh?" He looked back at her with a companionable grin.

Lydia nodded. There was no point in having to explain that her father's friend had come to Trubecke to meet her. And the driver's next question, one which he evidently had been wanting to ask her since she had got into his cab, made her glad that she hadn't contradicted herself.

"Say—none'a my business, lady, but ain't that a nurse's dress you got on?"

"Y-yes, it is. You see, I—I'm on vacation from a New York hospital, and my fr-friends in Trubecke invited me to stay with them, and their little boy needs someone to look after him——"

"I get it. Sure. That's nice, comin' all this way out here to do a good turn for yer friends." He gave her a smiling nod.

How easy it is to create a background for yourself that people will want to believe, if you do it from the start, Lydia thought to herself. By dint of a nod and a factual statement ambiguous enough to let the cab driver supply

114

his own interpretation of those facts, she had completely eased his earlier suspicion of her.

She rolled down the window, because the dry heat, even so late at night, had become oppressive. There was hardly a breath of air stirring. She looked out, and far ahead she could see a few pinpoints of light . . . in the houses bordering the edge of the town. A sudden exhilaration took hold of her, making her forget how exhausted she really was after the long, eventful day.

"That's Trubecke, isn't it?" she asked, knowing that it was, yet wanting, somehow, to have assurance that after this long journey which not much more than twenty-four hours ago had not even been a wishful dream, the town was not a mocking mirage.

"Sure is, lady. Say——" The driver's commercial instinct went to work. "——if you need a guy to drive you around tomorrow, I could stay over. Course, that's up to you. I'd give you a break on the rates, see?"

"That's very kind of you. But I'll be staying on for a while, I'm sure. Thank you, anyway."

"Oh. Sure. No harm askin', though, huh?"

"No, of course not, and it was very thoughtful."

Crestfallen a moment, he tried again, his face brightening. "Mebbe I could come by fer ya next week, huh? Or a coupla weeks from now—jist say the word."

But Lydia wasn't listening. Because she had just caught sight of the old white house . . . the house in which she'd been born and known happiness and love for twelve carefree years—till that day when her mother hadn't come back from that drive to Santa Barbara . . . till the harrowing experience of the trial in Bakersfield . . . till her father's mysterious disappearance and then Aunt Corinne's announcement of his death.

The house loomed far to her left, but was recognizable even under the hazy moon. The spired attic, the stately portico, the Gothic-styled windows. Under that haze, it was more a wraith than an actual structure, a phantom of grayish white isolation. Even eerier now than when she had left, for the houses that had bordered it as from a respectful distance had vanished, so that it stood alone, lonely and secretive, empty and yet full of ghosts and shadows.

The shadows of the past, the dark of memory, the brooding oblivion of laughter and happy voices that were no more—that was what it now sheltered. And, perhaps, something more, some unknown secret which, if revealed, would make the dark of memory darker still.

Chapter Seventeen

THE HOTEL was a three-story building of red brick and white wood, and the sun had turned the red to a dusty pink and the white to a dirty parched gray. It had forty-five rooms, and only when the paper box factory executives had come to town to hold the opening-day ceremonies for their new plant had it ever been filled to capacity.

"Here y'are, lady." The cab driver shook his head. "I know if it was me, I'd a stayed in New York. Betcha they sure got some snazzy hotels there, huh?"

Lydia took the brown envelope that the unknown phone caller had left for her at the airline ticket counter, and paid him the fifty-dollar fee she had promised. He took off his cap, grinned, nodded his thanks, and effusively put them into words as he got out to open the door for her. It was, Lydia reflected with the first flash of droll humor she had known since setting forth for Mrs. Burnan's on a new day which she was to end across the continent—an exit that would have greatly pleased Aunt Corinne who loved to have "menials," as she invariably termed them, make a fuss over her.

"Well, good luck! Now, yer sure you don't wanna have me come back later, huh?"

"No, you've been very kind and I'm most grateful. But I don't know what my plans are, and there's no sense having you make this long trip for nothing."

"Tell ya what——" He fished in the pocket of his uniform, came up with a dirty, crumpled card. "Here's where you kin call if you wanna have me run out. No bother. Any time, see? If I ain't in, jist leave word. My name's on the card—I had it printed at a reg'lar shop. Okay, then—well, good luck!"

"I hope so. And thank you again."

The slender girl moved towards the entrance of the hotel. Inside, there was a small desk behind which a bald little man dozed on a padded stool, his head resting on his folded arms. The lobby had a faded green runner on the floor, a nondescript potted plant in the wide glass window, two overstuffed armchairs that had seen better days, and a small couch that would never know a better one.

She opened the glass door and entered. It slammed noisily behind her, and the old clerk woke with a start, his jaw dropping, watery gray eyes bulging and blinking with alarm.

"I—I didn't mean to disturb you," Lydia proffered. "I think the Lawsons are expecting me."

"Oh—oh yes. That's right. They're up in 24 and 26, the second floor. The boys are in 26, I know, and they're asleep for sure. I'd better ring 24 and tell them you're here. What's your name?"

"Lydia Turner." The note had not told her to give any other name, and she could not see a reason now for hiding it. Besides, back home again after eight deviously channeled years, she was, more than she had ever been before, proud of her father's name. Consequently, there was not a quaver or any hesitation in the way she said it.

"Just a minute, Miss Turner. I'll ring up there, then."

She waited, holding her coat, her purse strapped over her shoulder. Now she would have been grateful for a bed, for fatigue was making her legs tremble uncontrollably, and her shoulders and arms were almost numb.

Lydia heard the clerk talking on the phone, but caught little of what he said. All of a sudden, the nervous reaction from the swift decision and the journey that had followed it had caught up with her, and she felt herself wavering, her eyelids drooping. She glanced longingly at the faded old couch near the window. She would have given anything to fling herself down on it to sleep without concern for the future.

The clerk was looking at her, talking: "It's all right, ma'am. Mrs. Lawson says you're to go up and get some sleep. They'll see you in the morning. Now if you'll register, I'll give you room 28, that's right next to the boys."

He was pushing the worn old register book at her and a nib pen. She dipped the pen into the old-fashioned ink bottle and scrawled her name across the page.

"The room number, too, ma'am, if you don't mind. And where you're from. It's rules," he said apologetically as he turned to the rack and took down a key. "Here you are, ma'am, and I hope you have a good night's rest."

"I'm sure I will." Lydia gave him a wan smile.

Then she slowly ascended the narrow stairway. The light cloth coat felt like a millstone, and even the moderate weight of the purse seemed intolerable. How her legs ached with each slow step! How good it would be to sleep, thoughtlessly, dreamlessly. If, at this moment Aunt Corinne had led her before a table laden with the most exquisite viands, the most subtle cuisine, the finest vintage wines, she would have found them tasteless. But the sheer, voluptuous anticipation of sleep almost made her throb with anticipation.

Another floor, step by slow, arduous step. Then, at last, the landing, and the dark hall, lighted by a single bulb at the far end. Dull, dusty-looking green carpeting, worn thin with years of endless scuffings from people taking the same track, for one could see the patches of a dirty tan material where the original carpeting had been worn away, making a kind of predictable pathway to the stairs.

Room 28, at last. Even stooping to insert the key in the

lock was physical exertion now. Her eyelids were so heavy she could hardly keep them open. There . . . the key turned and the door opened to her hand on the bulbous old knob.

The room was hot and musty-smelling, as if no one had been in it for years. Tired as Lydia was, she managed to pull open the window. Then she locked the door, took off her cap, then her shoes. Without bothering to undress further or to wash, she flung herself down on the narrow bed with its hideous pink cretonne cover, and, in a moment, was fast asleep.

Lydia was walking in the old house again. White sheets, like shrouds, covered the furniture. The old Gothic-shaped windows were dim with the accumulation of sun-baked dirt. The air was musty, too, like the hotel room. She was at the winding stairway, her hand on the banister, touching, remembering how she had held it while she pranced quickly down the stairs to meet her father at the door. She was turning to look at the door, but there was no one there. There was silence everywhere.

She knew the house was deserted because she had called out, and there had been no answer. Not even the ticking of the old grandfather's clock. But, of course, it wouldn't tick anymore. The heirloom was up in the attic, and kept out of sentiment, not for use. The attic—it would be empty too. Beckie and Gloria wouldn't be there. Beckie had said she wouldn't ever play with her anymore, and Gloria's parents had moved away. She knew because when she got to New York with Aunt Corinne, she had sent a postcard showing the Empire State Building, and the postoffice had returned it marked: "Moved—Address Not Known."

There was no one in the house but herself. And yet she had the feeling that someone was watching her, even though she couldn't see them. Was it a ghost, like the white sheet over that big armchair in the corner of the living room? She ought to open the windows, to let some air into this musty old house. But then the ghost might vanish. And then—there was a loud knock . . . and then another. There was someone at the door. Maybe— maybe it was her father—she turned, her face lighting, and she ran——

"Oh—just a minute, please." Lydia sat up dizzily, rubbing her eyes with her knuckles, groggy from sleep. She glanced down, saw that she was still dressed in the nurse's uniform. Then she remembered. She was in a hotel room. She had fallen asleep. But she had been dreaming. Dreaming that she was back in the old house, waiting for her father, and she had just heard his knock——

She walked unsteadily to the door and opened it. A woman in her mid-forties, of medium height, her attractive ash blond hair streaked with gray, her features round and soft, with ripe, smiling mouth, confronted her.

"I—I guess I must have been asleep. "Y-you're Mrs. Lawson?" Lydia stammered.

"I'm Marge, my dear. And you're Lydia." The handsome matron stepped forward and impulsively kissed her her on the cheek, affectionately squeezing her shoulders. "You don't remember me?"

"N-not too well, I'm sorry to say."

"That's understandable. I only came up with Jim one summer on his vacation to see you and your father and mother. And let me see—you were just four then. No wonder you wouldn't remember. But you'll remember Jim, I'm sure. I know he came up to visit your father almost every year till——"

Lydia searched the attractive, still youthful face for the completion of that sentence, her eyes dark and troubled. Then, when it wasn't forthcoming, she went directly to the heart of the matter: "Till my mother died—is that what you were going to say?"

Marge nodded slowly. "Yes, that's right, Lydia. Now, come have some breakfast with me, and I'll introduce

121

you to your two young charges. We had them rather un-expectedly, you see." She chuckled softly, her eyes warm and happy at the remembrance. "After we had John and Ray, we thought that would be all of the family. Then, about a decade later, when I'd just about given up hope, along came Michael and, two years afterward, Peter. Four boys. I'm very lucky."

Lydia smiled. This was something out of the shadows that engulfed the past that she could understand and hold to. The warmth and longevity of marital ties in which neither felt the slightest chafing restraint, but instead grew more infrangibly devoted to each other. The heartjoy of wanted children, each with a personality to contribute an inimitable gift of love to the family.

But then the swift dread of learning the reason for this journeying back into time made her smile fade, and she said, "I—I don't understand all of this. But a man called me back in New York and told me to come back here to find my father. He left money for my fare. But I've been told my father is dead—that he died a few months after Mother did. Marge, will you tell me what it all means?"

"Not till you've had breakfast, and then I won't be the one to tell it to you. Jim will. Freshen up a bit. Didn't you bring any luggage?"

Lydia shook her head. "No. I—I didn't want Aunt Corinne to know what I was going to do. I went right from work to the airport."

"Well, that's no problem. I'll be back for you in fifteen minutes, then we'll go to breakfast and you'll meet Jim. He's just a year older than your father, and he's your father's best friend. That's why he's here."

"I—I see," said Lydia, who didn't see at all.

Marge gave her a sympathetic look, the look of a ful-filled, life-loving woman who could sense someone else's feelings without being told everything in so many words.

"Not yet, you don't, honey, and don't fret about it. Time works everything out. That's what Jim always thought, and you'll see if he's not right. Now you go get ready. Hungry?"

So homey and genuinely concerned was the blonde matron's tone that Lydia was inexplicably affected; she almost wanted to burst into tears and cradle her head on Marge's shoulder. Nobody had talked to her so kindly since the days in the old white house. It took time to get used to it after the lengthy course of nagging she had had to take under Aunt Corinne. She forced herself to be as matter-of-fact about things as Marge was, and examined the latter's question. Come to think of it, she was hungry. And she didn't feel exhausted. The long sleep had done her good.

"I—I guess I am. Oh—what—time it it, Marge?"

"Half-past eleven."

"Oh my Lord!" she ejaculated.

"Now, don't you start getting unhappy about sleeping so late, Lydia honey, or I'll get downright angry with you. If I'd made the trip you did, I'd still be in the sack. And you're not holding us up. I've had my coffee already —instant, made right in my room. So has Jim. He's out taking a walk around town, just to get the feel of things. One of the taverns round here serves meals, we found out. That's where we'll have breakfast. So you take your time, hear?"

"T-thank you. I'm still in something of a daze——"

"Quit trying to make explanations, Lydia," Marge grinned. "I'll see you down in the lobby in about fifteen minutes, okay?"

Jim Lawlor was waiting for her in the lobby when she came downstairs. He rose to greet her; she saw a heavy-set man whose unruly hair was almost entirely gray, a jovial face with clear, searching eyes; he was almost six feet tall. Despite his bulk, he moved swiftly, and if it

123

had not been for the gray hair, she would not have guessed him to be more than thirty-five.

"Good to see you, Lydia," he greeted her with a vigorous handshake, grinning like a boy. "Let's go on down the street. Marge, unless I'm very much mistaken, has found a table and ordered breakfast. I hope you like scrambled eggs, Canadian bacon, fruit juice, and coffee?"

"It sounds like a feast, Mister——" Seeing his eyes narrow warningly, she added quickly, "—Lawson. You've a wonderful wife."

"I think so, anyway. I guess our four heirs apparent do too, unanimously. Let's go."

"I can't wait to——" she began, but stopped as she saw him put a finger to his lips and glance at the desk. The day clerk was a gangling young man in his late twenties, pimply, with touseled black hair long overdue at the barber's; he was chewing a toothpick as he lolled back on the stool; his beady brown eyes were covertly studying them.

Jim Lawlor walked to the door, opened it for Lydia, then followed her down the street. As they began to walk, Lydia saw a man coming towards them. He was nearly bald, only an inch or two shorter than her companion, and dressed in a khaki shirt and tight khaki trousers. The shirt was open at the neck, and the grizzled gray hair of his burly chest was as thick as that of an animal. The sleeves of the shirt were unbuttoned. His wrists were thick, their veins standing out, and his fingers were short, squat, heavily knuckled. His large-lobed ears protruded almost grotesquely; his face was round, the skin tightly drawn and darkly suntanned over cheeks and jaws, but a noticeably prominent dewlap at his throat hung like a desiccated growth and joined the beginning of a double chin. Incongruously he had a pure, chiseled Roman nose which hinted that in his youth he had been handsome; a deep wide cleft ran down to the fleshy upper lip. His eyes were widely spaced, deeply hollowed, and, as he neared them, Lydia shivered at the malevolence of the catlike green pupils, accentuated by the short sandy lashes and thin wavy brows.

Just over the left-hand pocket of his blouse, he wore a silver star. He was ambling, thumbs hooked into the broad black belt around his middle, and he wore no hat. Instinctively, Lydia moved to the right to give him room as he came closer to them. His fleshy mouth twisted into a smirk that passed for a friendly smile, and, without moving his thumbs from his belt, he inclined his head.

"Howdy," he said in a deep bass voice. But his eyes were on Lydia though he had addressed himself to the gray-haired man beside her. "See you got yourself a nurse, Mr. Lawson. Gonna be in Trubecke long?"

"As long as necessary for my business, Sheriff Hines," Lydia's father's best friend coolly answered.

The young brunette's eyes widened. If it hadn't been for the star, she wouldn't have recognized Elwell Hines. Eight years ago, he had been at least forty pounds lighter, without the double chin and dewlap, and he had had a thick shock of sandy brown hair.

Chapter Eighteen

IN THE BOOTH inside the little tavern at the corner south of the hotel, Lydia remarked to Jim Lawlor on her surprise at the changed appearance of the man who had arrested her father on the charge of having murdered her mother. A wizened little man with spectacles and a sparkling clean apron brought them their breakfast; he then discreetly retired to the back of the bar, where he began to polish glasses with an industry that belied his age.

Jim Lawlor poured a generous dose of granulated sugar into the strong black coffee and stirred it with a spoon, his face grave and thoughtful.

"Good living can do that to a man sometimes. That and worries."

"Worries?" Lydia echoed.

He nodded. "When a man comes up in the world after a hard start from scratch, and then comes into a windfall, he's likely to get a split personality. Half of him is glad about it—the other half is afraid it'll be taken away from him. I've seen it happen lots of times in the movie industry back in L.A."

"Mr. Lawlor—can I call you by your real name now? All this mystery is too much for me. Won't you—can't you, tell me what it's all about? Is my father still alive?"

Jim Lawlor and his wife exchanged a questioning look, then Marge slowly nodded and said, "She has to know sometime, Jim. That's why we came here."

"All right, Lydia. I'll tell you all I can." Jim looked at

the young brunette unsmilingly, but his eyes were warmly sympathetic. "Yes, your father's still alive."

"Oh, thank God!" Lydia exclaimed, and then burst into overwrought tears.

"Let her cry, Jim," Marge Lawlor murmured. "She's overexcited and it's best for her to get it out of her system before——"

"That's enough, Marge honey. I know what I have to do," he interrupted. "Finish your breakfast. Are the youngsters okay?"

"As always, you big lug. I came down here while you were still pounding your ear and brought them up some toast, jam, milk, and cereal. Seems like this tavern gets what restaurant business there is in Trubecke these days. They're tired of being cooped up in that hot little room; they're eager to meet their new nurse."

Lydia fumbled in the pocket of her uniform for a handkerchief, blew her nose, sniffed, and blinked. Then she looked up wonderingly at the handsome matron.

"Then what that man back in New York told me on the phone is true?"

"About Peter and Michael? Oh, yes, Lydia, honey," Marge chimed in before her husband could answer. "You see, Jim's become a kind of star reporter for the L.A. *Times-Examiner*—from the way he brags, I hear tell he's in line for an editorship one of these days. And even if I am forty-five, having those two youngsters has made me feel like a girl just out of college all over again." She shot her husband an affectionate wink. "I like to go places and do things and not be kept in the kitchen and the nursery. Besides, Jim's had to work hard on his job to get where he is and he hasn't had much time to play. So we've been experimenting the past few years trying to get a kind of governess for the boys—Ray and John are old enough to go out and get married if they've a mind to, you see, so we can catch up on some of our

127

nightclubbing and such. You've got a job for yourself with us, if you want it."

"Yes, but——" Lydia began, more and more bewildered.

"Let me tell it, Marge."

"You've got the floor, Jim."

He leaned forward across the table, his eyes intent on Lydia. "Let me fill you in a little, Lydia. Marge is right about the nurse angle. It sort of dovetails with giving you a reason to come out here. Me—I've been spreading it around town that I used to have an old friend here; that my health's been shakey lately; and I've been thinking of retiring and maybe putting my money into a business. Maybe one like that paper box factory that folded up."

"I—I see."

"How did you sign the hotel register, Lydia?"

"Why, with my right name. Shouldn't I have?"

Jim Lawlor shook his head, his lips tightening in a sardonic smile. "You did exactly the right thing, honey. Unless I very much miss my guess, our high-living sheriff was moseying down to the hotel to look at that register and see who the cute young nurse is. It ought to give him something of a start."

"Sheriff Hines? But—but he was always nice and pleasant, even when he—even when he had to take my f-father in that time——"

"I've no doubt of that, Lydia, honey. But I'll lay odds that he's got a mean streak in his nature. You don't put in over twenty years in the newspaper game without having a seventh sense about people when it comes to sizing them up on a quick impression. But let's get to the point. I told you your father's alive. That's true, Lydia. I can't tell you everything yet, but I will ease your mind all I can so far as what I'm supposed to tell you."

Lydia shoved away her half-empty plate, leaned forward, her eyes imploring. "I—I want to know so much —I want to see him. When can I see him, Mr. Lawlor?"

"Not yet. It still isn't safe. It may not even be safe for you."

Now his eyes were hard, probing, and his voice had lowered. Again Lydia felt an inexplicable chill surge through her. "Not safe for me?"

"No. Your father asked me to find out if you've courage enough to play the bait in a little game."

"Mr. Lawlor, you—you're driving me crazy." She burst out impetuously. "I want to know what's going on: why my father can't show himself—I—it's not a game for me, I assure you! For eight years, I've been in New York with my aunt, believing that both Father and Mother were dead—not knowing what I was going to do with my own life. With no warning, someone calls me on the phone and tells me Father is alive; he leaves money for me at the airline ticket office so I can come out here, following all sorts of strange instructions. I'm not very good at games any more—all I know is, I love my father and I want to see him—or at least have proof that he's really alive. So far, it's all been talk." And then again she burst into racking sobs.

"Take it easy, Lydia," Marge soothed. Then, her voice sharp as she turned to her husband: "You're a swell explainer, you are! Don't you know anything about the opposite sex? Her nerves are on edge; they're twisted into knots by all this mystery. Now start in at the beginning, even if you aren't supposed to fill in all the gaps."

"All right, all right! Don't crowd me, woman," Jim Lawlor leaned over to give her a propitiatory peck on the cheek. "Lydia, I'm sorry; Marge's right. Now, stop crying and listen. In a little while, I've got to go down to the bank. I'm still playing the unhealthy, retired businessman who's thinking of investing money in Trubecke industry—God knows this town needs it. It's dying on the vine. From the talk I hear, if something doesn't happen pretty soon, a lot of native residents are going to pull up stakes and try their luck elsewhere. There, now, that's better."

Lydia had again dried her eyes, taken a sip of her cold coffee, and composed herself. But the fixed intensity of her gaze betrayed an almost frantic supplication.

"How about some hot coffee to steady your nerves?"

"No. Please——" Her lips hardly moved as she kept looking at him.

"Then, here it is, as much of the story as I'm allowed to tell. Your father and I went to college together back in the Midwest, and we were quite good friends. I came out here ahead of him, landed a job in L.A., married Marge right quick and had Ray and John, and got involved with my newspaper job. You know, I think, how your father came here because of his health and worked on the *Reporter*?"

Lydia nodded. She sat, hands clasped under her chin, leaning forward, her body taut, absorbed in every word.

"We kept in touch every year. Marge came along once with me, but you were too small then to remember her now. Sometimes, your father and I met in L.A. or Frisco, once in a while I came to the house. You used to call me Uncle Jim——"

"Yes, I remember—you—you've changed a little——"

He gave her a wry grin. "All of us do, when things go well for us. Just like the sheriff. I put on thirty pounds, got gray, and fuller in the face. But you've changed, too. You used to be a lanky kid—now, you're a beautiful young woman. Anyway, to get back to the tale, I heard about your mother's death so I phoned your father. He told me that he was very worried because things had been going on in town he didn't much like. He had a feeling he'd be blamed for her death—and, as you know, he was. I helped him get a lawyer in Bakersfield. There wasn't any real evidence he'd killed her, so they let him off. He told me he was writing another novel, a kind of morality play as in the olden days, with hidden meanings, and that it would set down what he felt was happening."

"Is—is that what that man on the phone told me to look for in the attic?" Lydia could contain herself no longer.

Jim Lawlor slowly nodded. "Yes, Lydia. He told me at the trial he was going to try to finish it—but, if he couldn't, he'd try to hide it someplace where those who really loved him would find it. Even if they didn't— well——" He shrugged, looked down at his plate. "I think he had a premonition something tragic was going to happen. Then it did. I got busy on a big feature story about dope being smuggled in from Mexico, and lost track of him. Next thing I knew of him, your father had been reported missing after an auto accident. His car was found smashed and burned in a ravine about thirty miles southeast of Webster, but they didn't find the body— just blood on the seat—and his torn shirt, covered with blood, too."

"Oh, God——" Lydia buried her face in her hands.

"Then I learned you'd gone East with your Aunt Corinne. After that, there were only a few scattered follow-up stories in the L.A. papers. They still hadn't found his body. Finally, there wasn't a word about him, and a year went by, so I gave him up for dead, too."

Lydia raised her tearstained face, her eyes were beseeching.

"Later, I read that your Aunt Corinne had started proceedings to have him declared legally dead. It takes seven years, you know—the Enoch Arden law. And the seven years are up this month . . . specifically, a week from today."

"But, if he's alive——"

"I tell you he *is*, Lydia. But it was only six months ago that he knew he was Arthur Turner."

"Wh—what do you mean?"

"Your father was lured out to a lonely unused road by

131

someone who wanted to murder him—very probably the same murderer who killed your mother."

"Oh, God! Mr. Lawlor, who could have wanted to do that? She was so gentle, so good, she never hurt anyone——" Once again, tears ran down Lydia's cheeks.

"I've just a little more to tell you, Lydia. I can't supply all the pieces of the puzzle yet, first, because I don't know them; and, second, because your father made me promise to tell you only what he thought best for you to know at this time."

"I—I'm listening. Oh, please tell me how it happened——"

"He, himself, can't be sure. You see, he was badly beaten up and left for dead. But he didn't die. When the car was rolled down into the ravine with him in it, apparently he was thrown out alongside it. The car burned, and the people who tried to murder Arthur thought sure he was pinned in the wreck and left for dead. By some miracle which even he doesn't remember, he was saved—maybe by some farmer happening along by accident on a road nobody usually took. As I say, not even he can remember. You see, he's had amnesia all these years. Six months ago, in New York, while leaving his publisher's office, he turned his ankle and fell down some stone stairs and struck his head. He was in the hospital for two weeks. When he was released, Arthur knew who he was. He remembered only driving out in the car and being stopped by two masked figures, and then—blackout."

"Dear God, how horrible! My poor father! But—but he's all right now? He's well?"

"Well and successful. In fact, he's a famous novelist . . . under a different name. That part of his life is back in the shadows now, except that in the hospital they looked in his brief case and found a newly printed copy of a novel called *Winnow the Harvest* by John Doeson. That was the name your father took, the name by which he's known today." Jim Lawlor chuckled mirthlessly. "I suspect he took the name of John Doe, which is legally used to designate a person unknown, and added the 'son' as a kind of gallows humor. But that novel is a best-seller and his publisher is about to make a movie deal on it. The money's to go to you—he's made a will to that effect."

"All I want is to have him back," she impatiently broke in.

"And you will, Lydia. You see, he's been able to do some checking through a private detective agency. When he regained his memory of who he really was, and then the doctor at the hospital let him know what had been found in his brief case—some letters from his publisher helped, of course—he started to search for you. That was why one of his friends phoned you in New York and had you come out here. And he got in touch with me and told me what he had suspected. He asked if I'd be on hand to help you when you got to Trubecke. I just arranged to take my vacation earlier, that was all—no problems."

"You don't know how grateful I am for that, Mr. Lawlor."

"Shh! For the time being, let's go on using my *nom de plume*, as it were." He chuckled again. "You know, it's sort of fun to play counteragent at my age. And there's also a selfish angle to this whole affair—if what your father and I think is going to happen really does, I'll be on top of a scoop, which won't do me any harm on my job. Now, how about going back to the hotel and meeting your two new charges, Michael and Peter?"

Chapter Nineteen

TEN-YEAR-OLD Peter was fair like his mother, with big inquisitive blue eyes, chubby, a huge cowlick of hair constantly tumbling down over his forehead, and a bundle of nervous, chattering energy. Michael, two years his senior, was tall, slim, reticent, brown-haired, and soft-spoken. When Marge knocked at the door of their room, Michael opened the door, then turned back to chide his brother:

"Now you behave, Pete, hear? There's company."

"Come on out, you two." Marge laughed as Peter flung himself into her arms and gave her a big hug and a noisy kiss. "Here's your new governess—Miss Turner."

Peter, still clinging to his mother, cocked a quizzical blue eye at her without leaving the comfortable security of his mother's arms.

"Are you nice to kids?" he queried, and Lydia had to giggle at the wariness in his voice.

"Of course, she's nice, Stupid, can't you tell by looking at her?" Michael grumbled. "Don't mind him, Miss Turner, he's awfully fresh. I'll help see he minds you okay."

"Thank you, Michael. We'll get along fine. No, Peter, you don't have to worry, I'm very easygoing and I love children." Lydia's face again took on that radiant look she had revealed to the little girl at *L'Armorique*.

But Peter clung all the more tenaciously to his mother. "Huh," he retorted, "I'm not children, I'm ten going on eleven, that's what."

"That's right. You're almost a man. And I'm going to treat you like one," Lydia laughed softly, and held out her hand. "Shake on it?"

The grown-up gesture won Peter's heart. He ran to Lydia and hugged her, announcing in a delighted, high-pitched squeal, "Hey, Mom, I like her! She's nice!"

"Good," Marge complacently declared. "Now that that's settled, I supposed you two would like to take a ride with us."

"Gee, yes. Where are we going?" Peter eagerly demanded.

"Oh, around the country, that's what. Come along. Daddy's going to drive."

Jim had stayed down in the lobby, smoking a cigar and reading the latest issue of the Trubecke *Reporter*. He rose from the chair with the quick poise of an athlete as Marge and the two small boys and Lydia came down the stairs. "All set?"

"Can we have ice cream?" Peter wanted to know.

"I guess so. If we don't find a place out in the country, we can always get it back here down at the corner, Pete, old sock. Besides, you just had breakfast."

"I know, but I'm hungry again." The chubby blonde boy answered with incontrovertible logic. Marge turned to Lydia and rolled her eyes. "You'll have your hands full with that one, I'm warning you in advance. If he acts up, just smack him. Jim and I were both brought up to mind our *P*'s and *Q*'s when we were kids, so our own inherited the system from us. You hear that, Peter? I've just given Miss Turner permission to punish you when you get naughty, so don't try to see how far you can go with her, the way you did with poor Miss McNally." Then, to Lydia, "You see, the last few years Jim and I've wanted to travel and see a little of the world. The older boys, Ray and John, manage beautifully by themselves. Ray's staying on at U.C.L.A. for summer post-graduate courses—he wants to be a sociologist. And John's already been working for two years as a copyboy and occasional cub reporter on Jim's paper, though I assure you no nepotistic pull was used to get him that job. He was graduated top of his class in journalism, and the newspaper always gives the valedictorian a year's trial if he wants it."

"That's wonderful."

"Yes, we're very proud of him."

They were walking down the street towards the service station and garage where Jim had parked his Ford station wagon.

Marge continued, "But, as I started to say, we've wanted to have fun and a kind of second honeymoon, so the past few years we've left Peter and Michael with a governess. Trouble is, we've had bad luck with the three we've had—they just didn't take to Peter—he's so boisterous sometimes. That's why, Lydia, dear, we sent for you, once we found out you'd had a year of training as a practical nurse and were good with children."

"How—how could you have known that?" Lydia gasped.

Marge laughed gently and put her hand on the brunette's shoulder. "You're very unworldly, darling, and, for my money, these days that's an admirable quality. Don't ever lose it. Jim told you that your father hired a private detective agency. Well, that's how they found out not only where you were staying, but also about your schooling and how highly Mrs. Davis at the Hospital of the Angels spoke of you. So you see, dear, no matter what else happens, if you like the children and they take to you, you'll have a permanent job with us—at least till they're old enough to look after themselves. But that's for later discussion, of course. It's useful right now just in giving you a reason to come back here—in case anyone wants to know."

Her face sobered as she said those last words, and, once again, Lydia shivered. *There was so much she didn't un-*

136

derstand yet. And so much mystery about her father's staying away from her. After eight years and his terrible accident, who could still want to hurt him?

"Here's the old bus," Jim genially remarked as they walked into the parking lot of the service station. A weatherbeaten metal sign hung between two poles at the corner, proclaiming to all motorists and passersby "Trubecke's Only Car Repair and Service Station. Pete Ward, Proprietor."

Jim Lawlor took out his wallet, extracted a cardboard ticket as a man in greasy coveralls walked up to them.

"How's she look?" he asked.

Lydia's eyes widened. It was Pete Ward, who had been Sheriff Elwell Hines' deputy eight years ago, and who had come to her mother's funeral, then had talked with her father. Then later he and Sheriff Hines had arrested her father. He wasn't wearing a deputy's badge. And though he had looked to be about twenty-five in those days, now he looked more nearly like a man in his late forties. He was still stocky, but the bulge of his stomach and hips wasn't due to muscles, but to fat. His short-cropped pale yellow hair had a noticeable gray streak here and there, and his gray-blue eyes squinted and had a sour expression, as if he wondered why he was stuck on a job like this in a dead town like Trubecke.

He shrugged in answer to Jim Lawlor's question. "Okay enough, I guess. Only that engine of yours is gonna give you trouble in this hot country, mister. If it was my car, I'd have an overhaul from carburetor to transmission, get me? Better yet, I'd trade it in 'n get me an Olds. One with air-conditioning for this kind of driving. You're from L.A., are ya?"

"Last couple of years, sure."

Pete Ward looked at the ticket in his greasy hand, cracked the thick knuckles of the other, thoughtfully pursed his lips. "You'n yer family gonna stay in Trubecke anytime?"

Jim Lawlor shrugged. "I just might. Been thinking of retiring—I'm a vice president of a novelty manufacturing firm. Might even want to try my hand at opening a little factory here, now that I've learned all the tricks of my trade, and seeing if I can't beat my competition. Pick up a few bucks without working too hard, while my family takes it easy."

"Yeah, sure." Pete Ward spat down at his heavy dirty work shoes landing a gobbet of tobacco-dark saliva just an inch past the right toe. "This town could sure use some new dough'n business, lemme tell you, Mister Lawson. Ever since that paper box factory pulled out, we've had lean times here. There's talk about doin' some diggin' for copper, like old Augustus Edwards struck it a helluva long time ago, but nuttin' ever come of it. Yeah, it'd be good." He paused, shifting the cardboard ticket in his calloused, dirty palm, then squinted at Jim Lawlor. "How'dja happen to pick a dump like this, Mister Lawson?"

"Used to know a guy that lived here. Thought he might still be here. Just came down on a hunch—my wife and family and I are on vacation."

"Oh. Yeah. Sure." Pete Ward took out a plug of chewing tobacco, bit off a generous chew with big strong yellow teeth, worked it back and forth. "I know most'a the people in town. Born here myself. What was his name—this friend'a yers?"

Jim Lawlor stared hard at the ex-deputy for a moment. Then, without changing expression, he replied, "Turner. Arthur Turner."

Pete Ward's eyes widened, a cunning gleam brightening them for an instant. Then he shrugged. "That hunch of yorn wasn't so hot. Hell, Mister Lawson, Arthur Turner's been dead eight years. If he was such a good friend'a yers, how come you didn't know?" His voice was heavy with distrust.

"We lost contact after we left college. Last thing I'd

138

heard, he worked for the paper in town here. Then I got transferred East by my firm and only just got back last year. By then I was ready to retire. So, as I said, I came out here just on the chance I'd find him. We were going to motor on up to San Francisco for a couple of weeks, then maybe come back here if we can get what we want."

"Yeah. Well, it's tough about your friend. Darn tough."

"Those things happen. We were pretty good pals in college—you know how it is."

"Naw, I never was that lucky. Not enough to get to college. But I do okay. When I want some fun, I take off for Frisco or L.A. Or maybe Tijuana. A guy don't need college edjacashun for that, get me, Mister Lawson? Just dough. Well, now—sure hope the bad news about your buddy won't stop you from puttin' some 'a yer cash into this town. Like I said, we can sure use it."

"I'll think about it, of course. I've got to talk with a few people, you understand. The bank, for sure. You know who's boss over there?"

"Old Jonathan Edwards opened it. Everybody knows that. Left it to his two daughters—the younger one, Marcia, married this friend'a yers, Mr. Lawson. She passed on just a few months before your friend did, matter of fact. You see Carl Horley, he's the guy that runs it now. Not that it's much to run these days, after that factory closed down. Most'a the farmers go over to Webster Trust 'n Savings, see? Well, she's ready to roll if you are. I s'pose you wanna have me save you the same parkin' space if yer gonna be 'round here a spell, huh?"

"I'd appreciate it, thanks. Come on, Marge, Lydia, get in. I think we can ride three in the front seat. Let the kids get in the back. I can cope with their backseat driving, but not with Marge's."

"Well, I like that!" Marge feigned annoyance. "Listen to who's talking. When I'm at the wheel, Jim never stops telling me what I ought to have done."

Lydia gave her a warm, sympathetic smile. The good-natured banter between them, the contrast between exuberant Peter and sober Michael, had already eased some of her tensions, made her appreciate once again what closeness there could be among the members of a family where there was love.

The station wagon pulled out of the parking lot and headed out towards the distant mounds of the hills . . . towards the old white house, Lydia knew. In the back seat, Peter was pointing a chubby forefinger and shrilling questions to which Michael was replying with admonitory "Shhh's."

Marge glanced at Lydia, who sat next to the door, and smiled, taking her in as one of the family with that acknowledgment. Then she turned to Jim and said, in her casual tone, "You know, Jim, it was funny back there at the lot."

"What was, Marge, honey?"

"How he was calling you Mr. Lawson. You didn't tell him our name at all when you parked the car there day before yesterday, yet he knew it already."

"I know," Jim Lawlor replied expressionlessly as he steered the big car past Main Street and turned along Hinner Road. "He found out from the hotel register. And he's had help, too, I'd guess. Why do you think I purposely told him I was looking for Arthur Turner?"

"I wondered about that, myself." Marge admitted.

"Because, unless I'm very much mistaken, dropping that name is going to set off some action when it gets back to the right channels. Lydia, I told you a little

140

while ago that your father wanted you to play a kind of game where you'd be the bait, and he wondered if you'd have the courage. Well, that's why I let Pete Ward know why I really came to town. He'll get back to the sheriff, and from then on in you can expect to have the people responsible for what happened to your parents try to prevent justice from being done."

Lydia stared at him uncomprehendingly. "But, Mr. Lawlor, how do I fit into this?"

Jim Lawlor briefly glanced over towards her, his eyes narrowed. "It's very simple, Lydia. If your father's legally declared dead and you happen to be out of the way too, then all the money—and the land—reverts to your Aunt Corinne."

"The—the land? I didn't know about any land."

"When Augustus Edwards staked a claim to those hills to the west of your house in the days when he mined the copper that made him a wealthy man, he bought some of the land nearby, thinking there might be more copper. Apparently they never found any, but in those days they didn't know about certain other elements that are vitally important in our modern times—such as uranium, the stuff they use nowadays to make atom bombs."

"Uranium?" Lydia gasped.

Jim Lawlor nodded. "You own the land when you're twenty-one, Lydia, and the money your parents left—assuming them both to be dead. And if you were dead too, the only other living heir would be your aunt. There's just a week left before the hearing on your father's legal status. But, so far, nothing can be proved. You can help prove there was a crime committed— several crimes, in fact—if you're willing to go to the old house and look for your father's manuscript."

"I—I'll do anything that would help my father. Anything."

"Good girl! At night and alone. You're to be the bait for the tiger. But you won't be all by yourself. Others,

141

like me, will be watching both the bait and the tiger. And you'll have to trust me and do what I say."

"Tell me when and what I'm to do, Mr. Lawlor."

"Not tonight, but tomorrow night. Right now, we're going to look at the house and have ourselves a pleasant drive, and then get back to town and start seeing what sort of a commotion we've been stirring up for ourselves. And, meanwhile, it'll give you a chance to get better acquainted with Peter and Michael—Mrs. Davis in the New York hospital told the private detective that you've a wonderful way with children. I understand you read beautifully."

Lydia flushed with pleasure. Yet at the same time, a curiously fatalistic feeling took hold of her. all these past months, without her suspecting, inquiries had been made about her, plans prepared and perfected, machinations involving, not only her, but others whose lives and intentions she didn't even know. It was as if a deus ex machina had reached out of the past, without warning or previous intimation, plucked her up and set her down in Trubecke to resume the only life she had known till the tragedy of her parents' deaths.

And she would be the catalyst, the bait, which would set that deus ex machina into inexorable motion.

Chapter Twenty

In the early afternoon sun, the old grayish white house did not look formidable or terrifying: it had an air of desolation, seen from close by. Jim Lawlor slowed the station wagon so that Lydia could see it and recall its entity—though she had never really forgotten it. Yet she had never before seen it as it now appeared: the portico was badly in need of paint; the steps sagging and cracked; a jagged hole gaped in a living room window which might have been made by a stone thrown at it; there was even a broken pane in the narrow attic window from which she had so often looked and pretended to see Indian bands riding in attack, or a glittering processional of uniformed soldiers with swords and shakos. The front door stood slightly ajar, and on the porch were strewn torn newspapers, bleached yellow from the hot sun; a huge tumbleweed of combined gritty earth and withered vegetation edged into a corner of one of the steps.

Now Lydia could see that it stood virtually alone in almost half a mile of ground in its gaunt, still imposing structure. It had always been the highest house in Trubecke; now it was like a deserted tower in a desert. Frame houses which had bordered it for that radius of half a mile had disappeared, torn down for salvaged lumber, Jim Lawlor had said, after their owners had moved away from the declining town. Between the back of the Edwards house and the squat mounds of hills to the west, there was nothing now save sun-baked, arid grayish brown earth, with sparse shrubs and wild buffalo grass, a dreary landscape under the pitilessly bright blue sky.

It was symbolic of what had happened to the town which was bereft of industry and the working capital and acumen of old Jonathan Edwards. Jim Lawlor had told her that Trubecke's population had dwindled to sixteen thousand, and that more families were pulling out every month. Drought, too, the past three years, had inimically attacked those farmers still valiant enough to pit their skill against the elements.

It was dark inside. Lydia could see just inside the partly open front door; and the contrast between the glaring sun which, like an x-ray beam, played on the steps and showed up every flaw of decay and crumbling paint and the foreboding gloom just inside the door, was ominous even in this reassuring daylight. To go there at night and search in the attic, all alone, with only the ghosts of the past to keep her company, would take courage, even though she was no longer a child. Fear of the dark persists at any age when the mind grows more imaginative and conjures up new, more sinister, wraiths than ever childhood knew.

"We'll go on over to Bakersfield after we've had ourselves a scenic trip," Jim Lawlor declared, "and we might as well have supper there. There's a specially nice restaurant at one of the bigger motels. Not to disparage the very accommodating tavern back in Trubecke, but the menu's naturally limited, and I think Peter and Michael would enjoy a change."

"I want ice cream right now," Peter piped up from the rear.

Marge giggled. "I don't think our youngest is going to be much of a gourmet, from all the signs. He'd be happy with ice cream anywhere in the world."

"I'm still kid enough to share his enthusiasm," Jim Lawlor chuckled. "Okay, Pete, old sock, let's have about an hour seeing the sights, and then on to where you can get sixteen different flavors."

144

"Golly, gee, that's good! How many can I have all at once, Daddy?"

"We'll see. That depends on how well-behaved you are back there. Seen enough of the house for the time being, Lydia?"

"Yes. It—it's hard to believe I ever lived here. It all seems so—so unreal now."

"And you won't have to live there again when this is over. You'll be able to pick and choose for a change."

"I want to be wherever my father is. Even if it's back in Trubecke."

Jim gave her a quick, commending glance as he put his foot on the accelerator. "Your father's going to be proud of you, Lydia. Not that he wasn't always. But you've managed to stay a fine person in spite of—influences."

"You mean my aunt, I suppose?"

He nodded, looking straight ahead at the road. "I'm just a good friend, and it's not my business to sit in judgment of anybody or anything. Except that, from the detective's report, you've been both a ward and a servant to your Aunt Corinne all these years. She's kept you under her thumb, and, of course, it was to her advantage to do that. But you've still got spunk and common sense, and you've managed to get yourself some training in a profession that, if need be, would enable you to earn your own living. In my book, you've come out of it better than could have been expected."

"I—I'd just about made up my mind, when I found that envelope at the ticket counter," Lydia confessed in a low voice, "that even if the story about my father's being alive were—well, just a story—I'd never go back to Aunt Corinne; that I'd find any kind of job, no matter what it was, and go on with my education so I could be a registered nurse."

"I can't say that I blame you much, even if all

145

this hadn't happened," Jim Lawlor replied. "I met your Aunt Corinne twice, as I recall, and I don't think I would have relished the prospect of being at her beck and call twenty-four hours a day for eight years myself, as you were. But let's forget about all that and concentrate on the scenery—though I must say it's not too appetizing. I'd be back in Chicago tomorrow if I were told that I had to live around here if I wanted to stay on the West Coast. But then I always was a big-city boy at heart. Your father was, too, I think. If his health hadn't gone bad on him back in Chicago, he would have stayed there. Then —well——" He let his voice trail off.

There was not only ice cream of sufficient flavor varieties to enchant Peter, but also a swimming pool at the motel. Jim Lawlor, by dint of a discreet bribe to the manager, got permission for himself and his family and Lydia to use it for a short time. And, in the cool clear water, Lydia felt, at least for the moment, her uneasy premonitions wash away. Then, once again dressed and refreshed, she went back with them to the station wagon. She distracted herself by watching from the window as Jim Lawlor drove slowly through Bakersfield, pointing out the chief attractions. And one of these Lydia did not need to have him point out: the rectangular two-story building of the courthouse where her father had been tried for the murder of her mother.

Michael wanted to see a movie advertised on the marquee of a theatre on one of the main streets in town. "Why not?" his father jovially acquiesced. "It'll kill time till supper. And there's nothing to do in Trubecke tonight. Tell you what—I've got to call my paper and check some facts on a feature story I'm going to do. Why don't you and Pete and your mother and Miss Turner see it? Then I'll come back for you in a couple of hours, we'll have dinner back at that motel where we swam, and then back to Trubecke. You mind wasting time at a movie, honey? You, Lydia?"

"You know I'm an inveterate John Wayne fan." Marge laughed. "But usually Michael likes complicated English movies. I'm surprised at his choice."

"Oh, Mom." Michael squirmed and blushed. "I like a lot of things other people like."

"Then there's hope for you after all, boy," Jim Lawlor chuckled, as he stopped the car. Lydia got out and waited for Marge to join her on the sidewalk, while Peter squealed his delight at this unheard-of afternoon which had brought ice cream, a swim, and now a movie in swift succession.

"I'll tell an usher to come and get you when I come back," Jim promised as he waved good-bye when he drove away. . . .

A fried chicken dinner, salad, and iced tea at the motel restaurant, which, like the movie, was blessedly air-conditioned, rounded out a day of what had been unusual relaxation for Lydia. It was fun to tell the waitress what she wanted, without having Aunt Corinne comment about the error in her choice and, as she had often done, countermanding Lydia's order and arbitrarily telling the waitress or waiter to bring her niece something else instead. To swim, to eat ice cream, to watch a movie without any demands made on her emotions, had been utterly satisfying. She hadn't done any of those things since she'd been a little girl back in Trubecke.

It was nightfall when they finally drove back to Trubecke. Peter was asleep, his head against his older brother's shoulder. Marge watched them both with a fond gaze. A quarter moon was out, and the sky was cloudless. It would be another scorching day tomorrow. As the station wagon swung down the deserted road leading past the desolate old white house, Lydia shivered again. It was dark now, ghostly, and the partly open door seemed to

147

hold out menacing invitation. Tomorrow night, Jim Lawlor had said, she would go through that door alone, accepting its eerie bidding to ferret out the past. Up that winding old staircase, then to the end of the hall at the left, opening the narrow little door of what looked like a closet, but which opened onto the even narrower stairway leading to the attic.

She turned to look back as it receded from view as the station wagon speeded up. It reached into the sky, alone, still defiant and proud of its lineage from the days of pioneering Augustus Edwards. Peter, asleep and dreaming some uncomplicated fancy of childhood, uttered a little gurgling laugh and squirmed about against his brother, who glanced down, lips twitching in a half-sheepish little smile, then put his arm round the younger boy's shoulders. Lydia sighed. That old house had been planned for a large family, for the laughter of happy children and parents who delighted in them. It had never known quite that. And now it never would. And tomorrow night, when she would go unattended into its musty, hot, abandoned rooms, it would be good to remember Peter's dream-laughter. It might help to banish the waiting ghosts. . . .

Jim Lawlor walked Lydia to the door of her room after he had seen Marge and the two boys to theirs. "Sleep as long as you like, Lydia. No special plans for the day. We might even repeat today's program. It seems to have done you a world of good."

"It—it was really wonderful, Mr. Lawlor. I haven't had so much fun since——"

"I know." His face sobered. "And I'll tell you a little secret. You've made two conquests—Peter and Michael. They're crazy about you. Marge just put Peter to bed and he woke up long enough to cock an eye at her and say, 'Don't let that nice Miss Turner go way now.' And Michael, in his quiet way, thinks you're real folks. You didn't try to make him talk too much—he's still a bit bashful and a bookworm, though every now and then he shows a flash of conventionality—like that movie this afternoon, for instance. So—thanks."

"Thank *you*. They're darling boys, the both of them. You—you have two other sons, didn't you say?"

"Yes, John might be down here. He's got a week's vacation coming from the paper, and I called him while you were at the movies. You'll like him. He's going to be a writer some day, and a good one. He's even writing some poetry."

"Like—like my father."

"Yes. He's the serious type, while Ray's more the extrovert. Anyway, I hope you'll meet both of them in due course. Now I'll wish you good night. Tomorrow we'll talk."

"Yes. And—thank you again for everything. For a wonderful day."

She unlocked the door. The room was stifling. She turned on the light and pulled open the window as far as it would go. Tonight, she'd take off her uniform and sleep in her slip. Why she'd brought along even that light coat for weather like this was a good question.

Then she stopped and caught her breath. She'd left her strap-on purse on the chair. But there it was on the floor in front of the chair. And it was wide open. Quickly she inspected it. The envelope with the rest of her money was still there—the hundred-dollar bill and her change from the trip hadn't been touched. Every penny was there. But the copy of her father's novel and her little prayer book were both gone.

Chapter Twenty-One

Lydia saw no reason to alarm her father's friend and Marge by reporting the theft from her purse that night. There was nothing that could be done; only those two books had been taken. And the morning would be time enough to discuss what had happened. Yet it was evident to the young brunette that her presence and, doubtless, her true identity were known and being stealthily observed by those as yet unrevealed enemies of her father's. For a moment she knew utter panic; Jim Lawlor had said they might even make an attempt to her life. She paced the floor, undecided. Then logic took over; if she were being watched, those watching her would want to know her reasons for coming back to Trubecke. And she knew now what the reasons were: the quest for that incriminating manuscript which her father had written, which might well contain within its pages the explanation of everything that had caused the disruption of her childhood home, the tragedy of her orphaned state, and her bondage for eight years to Aunt Corinne.

Thus far, she had done nothing, even if they had followed from afar unseen by her and the Lawlor family, to rouse suspicion. Tomorrow night, when she entered the old house—that would be the time. She would be the lamb bound to the stake to await the tiger's emergence from the dark jungle. Till then, the tiger would not show himself.

So she locked the door, took off her uniform, washed, and lay down on the narrow bed. Sleep was easier than she had thought. It had been such a pleasant, friendly day, so full of trivial little occurrences that, conversely, meant so very much and had taught her once again how a family could be happy. She wouldn't think about tomorrow night, or about the theft of the books. And, before she knew it, she had fallen asleep. . . .

Over bacon, eggs, and coffee in the little tavern the next morning, Lydia told Jim Lawlor about the theft—about Mrs. Burnan and how the blind old woman had had her father's first novel in her library and had given it to her; and of how Aunt Corinne had told her it was trash. She told him, too, about having found the typed poem stuck under the candlestick after it had been missing for so long. When she had finished, he nodded gravely, and he used an expression that made her tense and quiver, for it was exactly the analogy she had thought of last night: "Look as if we're about to flush the tiger out of hiding, Lydia. That's good."

"I—I ought to have gone right back to your room and told you."

"It wouldn't have changed things," Jim said cryptically as he frowned and forked a mouthful of scrambled eggs. "And you're not to think I was overlooking any such possibility, or the possibility that someone might try to hurt you. I can tell you now—I sat up most of the night with a gun in my pocket, just in case, so you wouldn't have been in any danger. But I think you've guessed rightly that if there's going to be any action, it'll come only when you go back into that house and start hunting in the attic—they'll want to know why you're really here. They probably don't even know that manuscript exists. I'm sure your father never told anyone what he was writing."

"Can you tell me what it was?"

"No, Lydia. Even your father didn't tell me everything, and he has his reasons. He told me only what I've already told you—that it was a kind of fantasy in which he was putting down his impressions of what was going on. It probably isn't even evidence that could stand up in any court of law. But it's a link with that part of the past which involves his enemies, and they'd want to destroy it if they knew it was still around. They'd want to leave no trace of anything that could ever point back to them. And when they'd found it, if you were still here, then they'd try to do away with you."

"But—but that's horrible—all these years—to hate my father so much—just because he wrote some stories about people here and they didn't like what he said about them——"

"It's partly that, and it goes deeper than that. And what it is and was, you're going to try to find out tonight. You're not afraid?"

"Of course, I'm afraid. And for my father most of all. But I want to do it."

"Good girl! Now, you and I are going to take a drive by ourselves and I'm going to tell you how we're going to do it."

"I'll do everything you tell me to."

"You're not to worry. You'll be protected; your father and I are seeing to that."

"You—you think it—it's that serious, then?"

"I'm not going to scare you, Lydia. I'm not even sure of anything anymore. But if we're on the right track, your father and I, it could be—very serious, indeed. Now, finish your coffee and let's go take that drive. I'll drop Marge and the kids off at the motel in Bakersfield and we'll meet John there."

"Can I—can I ask just one question——"

"I can already guess what it is—is your father near here?" he finished.

Her eyes brimmed with tears as she nodded.

"Near enough to know and to be looking after you, Lydia."

"I'm ready now, Mr. Lawlor."

John Lawlor was already waiting for them in the lobby of the Bakersfield motel. He was six feet tall, wore glasses, his curly light brown hair and serious expression made him look like a college student working on his master's thesis. But his widely spaced blue eyes were warmly friendly, and his manners in being introduced to Lydia were sincere. She couldn't help flushing when he shook hands with her as she felt his firm grip and watched him smile. It wasn't one of those supercilious, impersonal smiles people affect when they're meeting a stranger and are just going through the motions of getting it over with so they can get back to their own important personal business. In a way, there was something about him that reminded her of her father.

"You're still on the payroll at the paper, I trust, John?" His father bantered once introductions were done.

"So they tell me. I'm getting the week off with pay, too, which ought to be a good sign."

"Yes, it usually is. Did you make that other call I told you to make?"

John Lawlor nodded. "It's all set. And I checked over the courthouse too, just before you got here. There's a hearing set for ten o'clock next Friday, Corinne Edwards, the petitioner, seeking to declare Arthur Turner legally dead for the purpose of settling the estate."

"Time's drawing short. Good work, John. Now, listen. Tonight, about eleven, Lydia is going into the house to look in the attic. I'm going to drop you off there on the way back. Pick yourself a good hiding place and keep my gun handy just in case."

"You think I'll need it, Dad?"

"Maybe not. Not if they used the same pattern they did before. And it worked for them twice—or at least they thought it did."

"You mean they'll try to let her find what she's look-

153

ing for, then grab hold of her and take her way out of town——"

"Damn it, you didn't have to spell it all out," his father swore, face darkening with anger. "Now, see what you've done!" For Lydia had started to tremble, her eyes huge and shadowed as they stared at Jim Lawlor and his tall son.

"It—it's all right. I'm still going through with it. I—I have to know what happened and how *they* are. You keep on saying *they* all the time. Then—then it isn't just one person?"

"No. It's much too big for one person. They're all in on it, and they've been very clever so far. Too clever. And if your father hadn't got his memory back by a lucky accident, they probably would have got away with it for good next Friday. We'll drop John off—don't feel too sorry for him, he's a good reporter and he enjoys being in on a scoop as much as I do. It'll be his first big one if it comes off. And he's got a plastic picnic bag with sandwiches and cold drinks so he won't starve or get thirsty, and a pocket chess set and a book of Ale-khine's best games to pass the time away." He started up the station wagon. "I've got to figure out a way of drop-ping you off at the house tonight, Lydia, without rousing suspicion that we know you're being watched. But, after I leave John at the house, we'll go back to Bakersfield and have ourselves a swim. What say?"

"Yes. I—I'd like that. I could even stand to see the same movie again, too—to get my mind off—tonight."

The sun had been high in the heavens when John Lawlor had got out of the station wagon, waved Lydia and his father a cheery good-bye, and calmly walked through the open door.

Now it was black night, and even the pale crescent of the quarter moon was obscured by drifting patches of

dark clouds. The heat had hardly abat~~
withering 100-degree mark of midafter~
breath of wind was stirring. Far to th~
flashes of heat lightning could be glim~
nous silence was everywhere, beyor~
stretching out on every side till it seemed that a..
world was concentrated into this bleak, deserted landscape and that there was nothing else.

Jim Lawlor had taken her back to Bakersfield and
they'd had that swim and seen that movie again, and
then had a leisurely dinner at the motel. Then he had ex-
cused himself to make a telephone call in the booth outside the restaurant. He had come out looking alert and
smiling. That morning before setting out from the
hotel in Trubecke, he'd made Lydia carry along her light
cloth coat. He had casually asked her whether it had
pockets on the inside, and she'd told him that there was
one deep pocket in the lining. Then he'd told her to
bring it along, so that she could put whatever she found
into that pocket.

After the phone call, he'd driven her back to
Trubecke and had gone to the service station. Pete
Ward was still on hand, in the office, tilting in a metal-
backed chair and sipping a bottle of Coke. He had taken
his time about coming out and he'd said it was a good
thing Mr. Lawson had come by just then because he was
just closing up. Jim had asked him to fill up the gas tank.

Then as he paid the ex-deputy, he had said, "Looks
as if I'll be going back to L.A. tomorrow. Might be back
in a couple of weeks if the bank gives me the deal I'm
after."

And Pete Ward had said, "That so?" as he took a rag
out of his back pocket and swiped it a few times over
the windshield.

Then Jim had lit a cigarette and said, "Lydia's going
to work for me, you know. Hired her as a governess for

today. But, before she leaves, I wanted her to see ˀuse where she lived. Sentimental reasons, natu-
rˀ."

And Pete Ward had nodded and said, "Sure, yeah, I know how it is. Ain't much left of that place any more. Don't know what's gonna be done with it." And then Jim Lawlor had added, after a puff at his cigarette, "Lydia used to play in the attic when she was a girl. She's sure she hid some of her favorite books and things in there, so she's going to look for them now. Sort of like going after buried treasure. Never can tell what you'll find when you've hidden something a long time ago."

And Pete Ward had given him a funny kind of grin and nodded and said, "Sure can't. Well, then I'll be lookin' to see you back here coupla weeks, huh, Mr. Lawson?"

And Jim Lawlor had said, "That's what it looks like. I'm going to run Lydia down to the old house now and leave her there. She says she wants to spend the night there. Probably the last chance she'll ever have to see what her old home's like, I imagine."

And then he'd started up the station wagon and waved to Pete Ward and driven on back to the old white house. And he'd given her a flashlight with new batteries that he'd picked up in Bakersfield and told her, "Remember, don't lose your head. You won't be in any real danger so long as you're in the house. And you'll be watched— John's there. And—well, just trust me—and your father. You're being well looked after, Lydia."

And he'd left her there standing in front of the old house, alone, carrying her light coat and the flashlight, and she'd watched the glowering taillights of his car growing smaller down the road till at last they disappeared and she was engulfed in the dark night. And now the black beyond the partly opened front door beckoned to her, and she was suddenly terribly afraid.

She told herself that the house could not be evil. Even if John Lawlor weren't in it, hiding somewhere, with

156

a gun to protect her, there was no evil lurking in those shadows. She had been happy there with her mother and father, and with Dolores and Inez. Even Aunt Corinne had been nicer to her in those days.

She took a deep breath, stiffening her shoulders, and then resolutely walked up the steps. They creaked beneath her weight, and again a chill of unreasoning fright traced its course through her body. But now she was on the porch and approaching the door. Boldly she pushed it open, wide open, trying not to shiver as she heard the rusty bolts and hinges squeal in protest at this rude invasion.

Then, snapping on the flashlight, she directed it at the stairway which she knew to be straight ahead. As she did so, there was a slithering sound, and a gray object darted past her; she uttered a stifled cry. Her heart began to pound, and she stood there, forcing herself to regain composure. It was only a field mouse or a young gopher, she told herself.

Now there was quiet, the quiet of a tomb. Beyond to her left, only dimly outlined in the blackness where the flashlight did not play, was the spacious living room, and the sheets over the remaining pieces of furniture vaguely loomed like apparitions summoned back at a séance, tenuous and ghostly; if she strained her eyes into that stygian darkness, she could even feverishly imagine that they were stirring now, coming to life after eight years of suspended immobility while time had halted for them till this renascence.

She told herself they were inanimate; for all she knew, John Lawlor might even be hiding there. And, raising the flashlight's beam, she walked towards the stairway and began to ascend the winding steps. Now, the old house seemed to come to life. At every step, she heard the creaking protest, like a hidden voice protesting her return. The banister was coated with layers of dust, and as Lydia momentarily turned the flashlight on it, she saw

157

fingerprints here and there along its ascending rail, preserved by the dust—or could they be freshly made? She could not tell, but at the thought, the pounding of her heart grew louder.

Now she was at the landing of the second floor. She knew her way now almost by instinct. The plaster was cracking on the walls, on the ceiling overhead. As she tilted up the beam, she shuddered at the sight of huge cobwebs—in whose centers some dark spiders seemed now to stir, resenting the light.

She had not remembered how the floor creaked up here as she neared the little door that led to the attic stairway. It was as if someone, invisible, were at her side, walking with her, so audible was each step she took, announced by the floorboards that seemed to yield so grudgingly to her steps.

There was the little door, its brass knob dull yellow and green with age and oxidization, smudged with dust. For an instant, she could not bring herself to touch it. But now she was near to the goal of her cross-country quest, so, once again, steeling herself, she reached out for the knob and turned it. The door swung open, and the little narrow stairway loomed ahead.

She must remember, she told herself, that the low beams meant she couldn't stand erect in most of the attic. She had bumped her head many times, even as a child, near the window. The window was to her left. There was a huge old black trunk, its straps rotting and loose, right beside the window. It had contained some of her father's books from the midwest, papers and mementos, and he had even packed his old Remington in there before he had left Chicago.

She reached the top of the stairs, stooping forward to avoid the beam directly overhead. She turned to the right and aimed the flashlight in that direction. There was very little left in the attic now. Aunt Corinne must have sold or thrown away a good many things. Like the wicker basket in which her great grandmother's china had been kept, so rarely was it used. Augustus Edwards' wife had used it in this house when the house had been very new. But Jonathan Edwards' wife had bought a set of Royal Doulton in San Francisco and had never used the other set. And the old painted wooden rocking horse Lydia herself had used as a child was gone; so was the padded black leather footstool on which she had used to sit so often, drawing it up to the window to look out at the squat little hills to the west pretending that she was in the turret of the castle and that the soldiers of the wicked Duke were coming to besiege her.

But the grandfather's clock remained there, leaning against the farthest wall, its pendulum still gleaming behind the long narrow glass case. Its white round face with the ornate black numbers was naked, for the glass had been broken long ago, and the minute hand had been bent. You could see the hole where its key could be inserted to wind it, but even the key had been lost long ago.

What a beautiful old clock it was, even in its useless, broken immobility. The hour hand pointed to "3" and the bent minute hand had lodged between the "6" and the "7." Three-thirty. Had it stopped in the hot afternoon or in the darkest night before the promise of a purplish dawn?

Father had always loved the old clock. He had wanted to have it repaired, but Aunt Corinne had said it was broken beyond restoration and that there was no sense wasting money or effort on it, it was out of style, and valuable only as an heirloom because it had belonged to her grandmother.

The silence had crept up the stairway with her. There was not even the ghostly ticking of this abandoned clock to keep her company.

Then, from far off, the faint rumble of thunder sounded, and Lydia started nervously, dropping the flashlight. She knelt down to pick it up, and, as she lifted it, the beam shone on the pendulum in its glass case. There was something strange about the pendulum. . . .

She moved closer, keeping the flashlight directed at the long golden shaft with its semicircular, weighted ball at the end. And then she saw it.

The long body of the clock had been tilted at an angle so that, kneeling as she was, Lydia could glance upward into the top of the pendulum case; she saw the circular outline of what looked like a roll of paper which was thrust in such a position it would ordinarily be out of sight.

She uttered a stifled gasp. She knew, unerringly, that this was her father's manuscript which he had hidden inside the grandfather's clock. It was safe there, because, as an heirloom, it would not be disposed of; Aunt Corinne would have no reason to examine it, because she had no intention of having it restored. In all the house, it was the safest place to hide something not meant for others to see —not meant for others who——

Her mind was staggered by the enormity of what she had just been thinking. Father had hidden the manuscript so that Aunt Corinne would not think of looking for it there. Yet he knew that she, Lydia, had loved the old clock——

How did the glass case open? Was there a key or a lever? She had flung down her coat on the floor; the flashlight in her left hand aimed at the case, she put her right hand over the glass, smoothing it, going along the beautiful, veneered wood, seeking an opening. But there was none.

She leaned back, her knees aching. Again the rumble of thunder sounded, nearer this time, longer and more ominous. And a flash of lightning for a swift instant sent its eerie glow through the windows of the attic.

Wait—a tiny round knob around the right side of the case. She pressed it with her thumb and uttered an excited cry as the entire panel behind which the pendulum was housed moved forward, open and yielding. Carefully pulling it to the left, she reached up with her right hand towards the edge of that hidden sheaf of paper, grasped it, and tugged; she could not free it at once, so forcibly had it been wedged upwards. Setting the flashlight down on the floor, she reached her other hand up to grasp it, and, with both, she was able at last to drag it down.

Quickly, she glanced through it. There were about a hundred typed pages, hastily typed, with many errors and hardly any margins. On the first page, her father had typed at the top: *"These Graven Lines"* by Arthur Turner.

Lydia looked round for a place to put it so that she could read some of it. On top of that old trunk by the window, maybe. But, as she picked it up, standing up with her head bowed forward to avoid the overhanging beams, she heard the squealing brakes of a car. As she stood petrified, holding her breath in numbed terror, she could distinguish the sound of footsteps hurrying up the stairs at the front of the house.

Chapter Twenty-Two

Don't panic, Mr. Lawlor told you not to panic, whatever happens. John will be hiding, with a gun, to make sure they don't hurt you. They won't, not in the house. You're safe as long as you're in the house.

Lydia told herself that as she crouched near the door of the attic. The flashlight in her hand still burned, and she clicked it off. Maybe they wouldn't find her. If she were very quiet and they didn't see the flashlight, they might go away.

Had she closed the attic door tightly? Yes. If only there was a place to hide . . . that old trunk, perhaps. Maybe——

But there wasn't time. She heard them coming up the stairs, and her heart began to beat so violently she thought she would faint. The impulse to scream for help rushed to her throat, but she clamped her palm over her mouth. *Don't panic, he told you not to,* she repeated inwardly.

They had stopped on the landing now. And she heard voices. A man's hoarse and jeering. And another's drawling and slow. And then—a woman's. A voice she knew as well as she knew her own. Aunt Corinne's voice.

"She's got to be in the attic, Corinne." That was the hoarse, jeering voice.

"Maybe it's some sort of trap, Elwell. That guy Lawson—I don't trust him. He don't look like no retired businessman to me." That was Pete Ward's voice.

"I tell you, we can't afford to find out who Lawson is. Not with the hearing coming up so soon—all we've worked and planned for. Why did that stupid little fool

162

take it into her head to come back here? If I hadn't called that old woman she worked for and her nurse hadn't told me Lydia'd said she didn't think she could come the next time, I mightn't have figured out what she was up to. And then, when I saw that she'd found your telegram, Elwell, thank goodness, she was stupid enough to stick it back not quite the way I had it, though I never dreamed she'd go snooping in my desk——" And that was Aunt Corinne again.

"Well, the damage's done. That's for sure, Corinne. You always were a stupid know-it-all yourself, if you want to know" Sheriff Hines was jeering. "Why the hell did you keep stuff like that around, anyhow? And if you'd come through with those monthly checks on time as we agreed, I wouldn't have had to send you that telegram at all."

So—Sheriff Hines had been the mysterious "LEX" of that telegram Lydia had found that stormy night. But what did he have to do with Aunt Corinne, and what did Pete Ward know about it all?

"All right, stop arguing, you idiot," Aunt Corinne snapped. "She's not in the house anywhere, Pete's made sure. And it was a good thing he went looking."

"Yeah—sure was. Some young punk was hiding behind that couch in the living room. Thought I smelled something funny—like food. So I walk around real quietlike, till the smell gets stronger—'n there's this guy sitting down with his back to me. Good thing I got the sorta eyesight kin see in the dark. My maw always told me it'd come in handy—she didn't know how right she was." He gave a brutal short laugh.

"You didn't——" Aunt Corinne began.

"Naw, jist socked him with the butt of my thirty-eight. He's sleeping peaceful and he won't get in our way. Wonder who the hell it was?"

"We've got to find her and get her out of here. I told you it might be a trap."

"How could it be?" drawled Sheriff Hines. "She hasn't got any friends in town, no more than her uppity father did. And she doesn't know a thing. Even if she thinks she does, she can't prove it. Probably some tramp picked himself a spot to hang out for a while and Pete caught him, that's all there is to that. Let's get to that attic."

Lydia heard the door open, then the thud of footsteps coming up the little stairway to her hiding place. And now frantic terror seized her. *They'd found John so he couldn't help her. And what would they do to her now?*

The trunk, she thought again. If only she could get into the trunk and hide, the way children hid—— But there was no time. The door was flung open and a powerful flashlight beam suddenly blinded her. She dropped her own torch and stood, still stooping to avoid the beams, paralyzed and captive now, while the three of them watched her.

"Turn your flash on, Pete," Elwell Hines ordered. "There, that's some better. Well, now, Miss Turner, you're a long way from home, I'd say. Gave your aunt quite a scare, you did."

Lydia stared at him, watching his fleshy mouth curve into a hideous smile that aimed at ingratiation and was sinister instead. Aunt Corinne wore a green silk dress, a ridiculously insouciant blue felt turban hat. She was smiling too.

"So you've come back to play in the attic, have you, dear?" Aunt Corinne purred like a cat that sees a bowl of cream set down before it and is in no hurry to begin to savor the treat. "I wonder what you've found? Some of your old childhood toys, maybe? But no, you wouldn't come all the way back to this dying little town for anything so nonsensical as that."

"I—I wanted to leave you." Lydia's teeth were chattering, and only by supreme effort of will was she able to speak at all. "I—I couldn't stand it any more. I wanted

164

to go on with my schooling, so—so I could be a nurse and not—not have to go out with you to all those places where you—where you treated people as if they were dirt."

"Sounds like her father, kind'a, doesn't she, Rinny?" Elwell Hines drawled.

"Don't forget yourself." Lydia's aunt flashed, sending him a furious look.

He guffawed and slapped his burly thigh. "Still the lady lookin' down her nose at the peasants, huh, Rinny? I know, you'd like to forget the times you 'n me used to sneak down to Santa Barbara and spend the weekend in bed——"

"Shut your filthy mouth, you bastard——" Corinne Edwards was livid with rage.

"Okay, okay. Lydia here's old enough to know the fact'sa life, I figger. 'Sides which, she's a nurse. Nothin' wrong in going to bed with a man, now is there, Lydia? Specially when your Aunt Rinny had to settle for me because your father wouldn't give her a tumble——"

"I told you to shut your filthy mouth," her aunt hissed.

Lydia's eyes widened. "You—you——" Her voice choked in her throat.

Corinne Edwards whirled towards her. "I *what* you little fool?" she snapped.

"In my father's novel—the book you didn't want me to read—you—you were the duenna who—who tried to stop him from finding his true love——"

Corinne Edwards strode towards her niece and viciously struck her across the mouth. Lydia recoiled, stumbled, and sank down on her hands and knees, a little trickle of blood staining the corner of her swollen lips.

"Duenna!" her aunt sneered. "Your father paid for that. I was the one he ought to have married, not my stupid younger sister. I was the one my father always preferred, the one who had the brains and the breeding. He used to tell me that. Marcia was afraid of her own shadow, her head was always full of romantic nonsense, like poetry and such trash. Then your father came to Trubecke—I wish to God he'd died of his tuberculosis before he got here—and turned Marcia's head. He could have had me and the money and the land and the house—but no, he wanted her instead. He always thought himself such a great writer, going around writing those sly stories of his about people here. Like the sheriff and Pete and me —a *duenna* indeed! But now they're dead, both of them, and everything's mine."

Hardly knowing how she knew, Lydia gasped. "You had them both killed, didn't you? And you had the sheriff and his deputy help you."

"Hey, now," Pete Ward looked alarmed. "This ain't no good, Miss Edwards. We gotta shut her up for good."

"There's time for that," Corinne Edwards said in a cold impersonal voice. "First, we find out what Lydia was looking for in the attic."

"What's that on the floor?" Elwell Hines pointed his flashlight down at the scattered pile of typewritten sheets.

Lydia tried to scramble forward, but Pete Ward was too quick for her; with a spiteful chuckle, he stuck out his heavy boot and jabbed the heel at her shoulder, sending her sprawling. Then he bent down and picked up the manuscript. "Here y'are, Miss Edwards. Some sorta writin', I guess."

Corinne Edwards picked up her niece's flashlight, turned it on, and played it over the top page. "So, this is what Arthur was typing after Marcia died. We haven't time to read it now, you two. Let's get Lydia out of here."

"What do we do with her?" Elwell Hines drawled.

"She'll have an accident. Like Marcia's and her father's. Only this time, try not to bungle it the way you did her father's."

"Look," Pete Ward complained, "could I help it if

166

they didn't find his body? Elwell 'n me followed him that night when he got into his car and drove away, and we caught up with him near Webster. I conked him one, and Elwell poured a bottle of good whiskey all over him 'n the front seat, 'n then we drove the car over to that ravine and let it take him on from there. Hell, I could see it burnin'—how was I to know he'd get outa the car and crawl away somewhere?"

"You both ought to have made sure. Then we wouldn't have had to wait seven years to get the estate, just because they never found his body."

"You—you had my mother killed—y-your own sister," Lydia gasped.

Corinne Edwards shrugged. "Marcia used to be so smug. Always telling me how happy she was with your father, and that I ought to get married, too, and be as happy as she was. She was a simpleton. Besides, I didn't kill her."

"Don't whitewash y'self, Rinny girl," Elwell Hines' voice was menacingly hoarse. "Sure, mebbe you didn't fix the brakes 'n the steering wheel yerself, but if we ever get up against the law, you'll go to the gas chamber just as much as we will. You're the one asked me to get it taken care of—for the dough you were gonna divvy up. And next Friday, when Lydia's father's declared officially dead, we're gonna divvy. Only we're gonna divvy it *my* way, not yours. Mine and Pete's. We took all the risks, don't forget that. And besides, what you were gonna pay us don't quite include what we gotta do now about the only other livin' heir—if you know what I mean."

He stared down at Lydia, and she cringed at the cold malignancy of his beady eyes.

"Seems like an awful waste, though," Pete Ward scratched his head. "Purty filly'n all like that——"

"I see," Corinne Edwards cut in icily. "You'd like her around at the hearing Friday, telling all she's heard to-

167

night. It's bad enough I had to rely on Elwell because he was the only excuse for a man in sight—but you, you've got no brains at all."

" 'Course," Elwell Hines drawled, "a wife can't testify against her hubby. Pete's taken a fancy to her—mebbe she could marry him and——"

"No." Corinne Edwards stared at the young brunette who crouched, trembling violently, on her knees on the attic floor. The woman's small pampered mouth twisted into a vindictive grimace. "She's her father's brat and she's got all his crazy ideas. She'd find a way to give Pete the slip and go tell her story. No. There'll be an accident. And this time, both of you are going to make sure her body's in the car. Use yours, Pete. Then you can always say Lawson told you he was leaving Lydia out here and you were worried about a young girl like that being all alone in this godforsaken house, so you drove out to see if she was all right. And she was scared and got into your car before you could stop her and drove away at high speed—do I have to do all your thinking for you?"

"That oughta do it, then, Rinny. Okay. Let's get her out to Pete's car. Rinny, you better drive the other way back to Bakersfield, so you won't be seen. Then stay low till the hearing. C'mon, Pete. Get her coat, you can use it to wrap round her face like a gag, see?"

"No—stay away from me—my God! No, please——"

Lydia rose unsteadily to her feet. But the two men seized her, and Pete Ward, grabbing up the cloth coat, wound it over her head and shoulders, muffling her cries. Corinne Edwards held the sheriff's flashlight, pointing it down the narrow little stairway so that the two men could trundle the writhing brunette down to the second floor landing, then out of the house.

There were two cars parked outside the house, a battered old Chevie belonging to the ex-deputy, and a gleaming new Studebaker, rented by Lydia's aunt in Bakersfield. Elwell Hines got into the Chevie while Pete

Ward flung Lydia into the back of the car and got in and leaned over and held her down, still muffled in the coat. Corinne Edwards waited a moment, then nodded, and got behind the wheel of the Studebaker. She started the car and turned it to the south.

Half fainting, smothered under the coat, Lydia tried to get up. Pete Ward sniggered and planted his heavy boots on her prostrate body.

"Damn shame to waste stuff like this, though, Elwell," he ventured.

"You heard what we gotta do. Me, I'd rather have the dough Rinny's gonna shell out. You can buy yourself a service station full'a floozies then, if you're a mind to. Now, let's get on out to that fork in the road near Webster. Nobody'll be around for miles. This one's gonna be easier."

The Chevie backed up, then made a U-turn and headed down the road to the north. Lydia squirmed, trying to get her mouth and nose free of a clinging material of the coat. Sadistically, Pete Ward dug his bootheels into her thigh and back. Twisting her head, she felt the coat slip away from her face, and opened her mouth to cry out, feeling the dirty carpet of the car floor rub against her lips.

"Hey, what's that up ahead?" Elwell Hines suddenly growled.

"Looks like—hey, it's the Highway Patrol! Get back to Bakersfield!" Pete Ward yelled. A blazing beam of light cut through the darkness at them. With an oath, Elwell Hines wrenched at the wheel, and turned the Chevie around. But the angle was too sharp. Lydia uttered a shriek as she felt the car skidding. Then, as the car toppled over onto its side, the wheels spinning, she was plunged into a blackness deeper than that of the old house.

Chapter Twenty-Three

LYDIA SEEMED to be struggling up out of an enormous black void, with nothing to hold to. Yet, far beyond, though she could not see them, she knew there were lights. And voices.

And the voices were known to her, out of the dark of memory, yet they held no terror for her. Not like the three in the attic . . . in the attic so long ago. . . .

"She's coming to now."

Her eyelids were leaden weights that fought against her efforts to open them. She felt as if she were swathed in a winding sheet. So this was death.

"Lydia, darling. Lydia—can you hear me?"

"Just give her a minute or two, Mr. Turner," another voice warned. "The sedative is wearing off, and she's had a bad shock. A lucky thing there wasn't concussion. Lying on the floor was what saved her. The two men who tried to kill her weren't quite so lucky, I'm afraid."

"Are they dead?" *That voice—what was so familiar about that voice?*

"The Sheriff is. Ward has a broken arm and three broken ribs. But he'll live to stand trial."

"And—and you're sure Lydia's not seriously hurt, Doctor?"

"Very sure. We took xrays at once, of course. There —her eyelids are stirring. And she moved her head."

"I see—oh thank God!" *That voice . . . that voice was——*

Through the blur, gradually, faces came into view— the white walls and ceiling, the bed on which she lay,

170

bandaged and confined. That was why she had felt swathed. . . .

"Lydia. My own Lydia. I ought never to have let you go back to that house of hate."

She blinked her eyes. Now the focus was clearer. But she didn't recognize the face of the man who stood beside her bed, staring down at her, eyes wet and lips quivering. Or, rather, she did. Because it was the face of the man in the gray nylon suit, the man who had bumped into her at the East Side Terminal, the man who had been on the plane to Los Angeles and then had flown to Bakersfield with her.

"Your voice——" she quavered.

"Don't you know who I am, Lydia?"

"At—at the t-terminal in N-New Y-York——"

"Yes. And on the phone, to tell you to go to that terminal."

"You said—you were my father's friend."

He took her hand, very gently. "I didn't quite lie to you, Lydia. I never lied to you before. Maybe you'll forgive that one little fib."

"The doctor—said a name—my father's name——"

He nodded. "He said my name, Lydia darling."

"You—you're my father—but—but you look——"

"I wasn't as lucky as you just now, my darling. And I was nearly killed in that car eight years ago. All I remember is that some man was pulling me away from the wreck. He spoke Spanish, I think. And then——" He shrugged.

Her face was wet and hot. She was crying silently, and she couldn't stop. Her fingers moved, entwining with his, and tightened.

"Don't stay too long, Mr. Turner. She needs plenty of rest. But she'll be fine," the doctor said at the door. "That means you, too, Mr. Lawlor, and your son."

"Right, Doctor." Jim Lawlor was standing at the other

171

side of the bed. And beside him, his handsome young face pale and taut, was John.

Still squeezing her father's hand, Lydia turned her head slowly. "Did—did they hurt you, J-John?"

"Just a bump on the head. I was a clumsy idiot for sure. Gosh, I'm glad you're all right, Lydia."

Arthur Turner cleared his throat. "Jim, there aren't words to thank you for your help. I didn't even have the right to hope you'd back me up in this way. I wanted to do it by myself."

"That's what a friend's for, Art. Besides, I'm grateful to you. I got myself the kind of scoop that every good newspaperman dreams of. And all the human interest you could ask for."

"A-Aunt C-Corinne——" Lydia's eyes were fixed on her father's face. Yes, it was different. But the twinkle in his blue eyes was the same—there was no mistaking that.

"The police picked her up just out of Bakersfield. She made a full confession. If only I'd kept my wits about me more than I did, your mother might still have been alive. How much did Aunt Corinne tell you in the attic?"

"That she h-hated you because—you preferred Mother to her."

"I did." His eyes were rueful. "She did everything but fling herself at me. But I loved your mother. And one day she said something to me. I didn't pay too much attention to it, and I should have—about my learning what suffering was for something I hadn't done. That was when she was planning—your mother's accident."

"But those nights—when you—locked yourself up and typed——"

"I was beginning to piece together some of the parts of that puzzle, Lydia, darling. Corinne was having an affair with someone, though I wasn't certain it was Sheriff Hines. And then she went to Santa Barbara—of course, he was with her then, it gave her an alibi if she'd

172

needed one. And she phoned your mother—I'll never know what story she trumped up to get her to rush down there. But the Buick had been worked over the night before. Your mother loved to drive at high speed on a lonely road, and Corinne knew it. So your mother was killed. Then I went for a drive to think things over while I was working on that book. I thought maybe I could create a plot that would be so like the one they had dreamed up that it would make them give themselves away. But then the Sheriff and Ward forced me off the road and knocked me out—and, well, the rest is a blank, till I had that accident in New York. As for my face, Lydia, I must have had plastic surgery. And they tell me I've become a famous novelist under another name." He took her hand and lifted it to his lips and kissed it. "It's all for you, now."

Her eyes were still full of tears, but she had never felt so happy. At least, not since the days in the attic when she and her mother and her father were together in the old white house.

"I'm going to go now very soon, darling, so you can sleep and get well quickly. And then we'll talk—we've so much to talk about, and to plan. Where we're going to live and what you'd like to do. You needn't worry about a job if you don't want to. I've plenty of money from my books. And you will inherit your mother's estate—what's left of it, except for the amount your aunt wasted on high living in New York and her monthly checks to the sheriff. Of course, Ward got some of that money, too."

"The land—Mr. L-Lawlor said something ab-about ur-uranium——"

Arthur Turner smiled, a gentle, yet pitying, smile. "Yes. That's what started your aunt thinking about murder for revenge and profit alike. Jonathan Edwards took all the copper out of those hills. But on some of the parcels of land he had bought up, there were indications of ura-

173

nium. At least, that's what a mining engineer your aunt met in Santa Barbara and brought up here thought. He was wrong. Jim Lawlor had some experts assay that land a few weeks ago and they reported nothing there worth mining. One of nature's false alarms. All along, your aunt believed she was going to be a fabulously rich woman. The only thing that held up her plans was my being declared legally dead. If she hadn't been so greedy and eager to believe that engineer's report, your mother might be alive today."

Lydia's father bowed his head and was silent a long moment. "You know, Robinson once said, in his *Lancelot*: 'The truth we see too late hides its evil in our stupidity.' * I thought I could see the motives in what my neighbors did, when all the time I was blind to what was going on in the house where I was always considered a stranger." He kissed her hand again and turned to go.

Lydia lay back with a contented little sigh. Her eyes shining through the tears now. There were tears for her mother, who was finally avenged, and there was sorrow that only the years would lessen as she realized that there would be no such miracle to return her mother as there had been for her father. There was happiness in knowing that her father had found a fulfillment that had transcended the malignant envy of those neighbors who had branded him a stranger and a foolish dreamer. Through his writing, so contemptuously mocked, he had achieved a new rich life.

They would be together again, and she would have much to learn from him, and much to share. But she would not be dependent on him. Not even for love. She would be a governess to Peter and Michael. If there was to be any inheritance, she would use it first to continue her nursing studies so that she could be more than

* "Lancelot," reprinted with permission of The Macmillan Co., copyright 1920 by E. A. Robinson.

just an apprentice. She wanted to be the best she could. She owed her father that, because she was his daughter.

Her eyes were very heavy again. Lydia smiled as he stood at the door and blew her a kiss. Her hand rose tremulously and returned it. Then the door opened and closed.

It was so good to be at peace. It was selfish to feel this way. A nurse shouldn't be selfish. When she woke up again, there were things she had to do. First of all, she hadn't told John Lawlor how grateful she was for his having tried to protect her and how frightened she'd been when she'd realized he'd risked his life for her.

Elwell Hines and Pete Ward had had another crime on their escutcheon, too, though only Pete Ward would be left to make restitution for that and the murder of Lydia's mother and the attempted murder of her father. Both of them had terrorized Dolores and her niece Inez just before Lydia's father had been put on trial for the alleged murder of his wife. They had coached both of them to testify that they had overheard quarreling between Marcia and Arthur Turner. And Dolores, afraid for her niece even more than for herself, had agreed. That was why she had lied on the witness stand about hearing them arguing. But young Inez had not been intimidated; she had said that she could remember only their happiness together. And so the sheriff and his deputy had paid off Dolores and sent her back to Mexico, telling her that Inez would be sent on to join her when everything had blown over. But they had driven her to a desolate spot near Baja California, beaten and ravished her and then tied her with ropes and left her to die of thirst and heat. And all of this had been done according to Corinne Edwards' plan. She too would answer for that crime, since she had been its strategist.

Lydia's eyelids fluttered, and then closed. She smiled. She felt herself sinking back into the dark. But this time,

175

it was not the dark of memory flawed with nameless dread. It was the warmly comforting darkness she remembered when her father had turned out the lights and then come to kiss her as she lay in her bed in the old house where she had been born.